Sara swung peacefully in the hammock between the two trees. When she looked up all she saw were leaves and the blue, cloudless sky. Then, she saw Jasmin leaning over her.

"Comfortable?"

"I most certainly am. Care to join me?"

"Would love to."

They lay side-by-side. Sara put her arm behind Jasmin's back and closed her eyes. She was sure that at any second, she could fall asleep. The sun felt soothing on her face and a light breeze blew through the trees. Just when she thought she might drift off, she felt the soft pressure of lips against her own.

Private Passions

LAURA
DeHART
YOUNG

THE NAIAD PRESS, INC.
1998

Printed in the United States of America on acid-free paper
First Edition

Editor: Christine Cassidy
Cover designer: Bonnie Liss (Phoenix Graphics)
Typesetter: Sandi Stancil

Library of Congress Cataloging-in-Publication Data

Young, Laura DeHart, 1956 –
Private passions / by Laura DeHart Young.
p. cm.
ISBN 1-56280-215-1 (alk. paper)
I. Title.
PS3575.0799P75 1998
813′.54—dc21

98-13234
CIP

For my mother, Sara Elizabeth DeHart Young
June 20, 1931 to November 4, 1997
Your heart is safe. It beats with mine.

About the Author

Laura DeHart Young has four romance novels published with Naiad Press: *There Will Be No Goodbyes, Family Secrets, Love on the Line* and this newest, *Private Passions*. Her fifth romance novel, *Intimate Stranger*, will be published by Naiad in 1999. Laura lives in Atlanta, Georgia. When she's not writing for Naiad Press, she works as manager of internal communications for a worldwide information company. Her partner, Jerri, and her pug, Dudley, are her constant companions.

Books by Laura DeHart Young

There Will Be No Goodbyes

Family Secrets

Love on the Line

Private Passions

Chapter One

The elevator chimed and the doors opened slowly into the lobby of the 15th floor. Sara picked up her briefcase with one hand, while juggling the *Wall Street Journal* and coffee in the other. It was already 9:30 and she was running late. She took a left at the end of the hallway and stopped abruptly.

Bill was standing just outside the main door to their office suite. When he saw her he raised his arms and began gesturing as he talked, his limbs jerking like a puppet's. "Well, the Dove Soap creative concepts are behind. We needed the TV boards for this afternoon's meeting. Jill was supposed to be working on them, but Greg pulled her for the UPS client meeting this morning and didn't tell me."

Sara nodded as she passed, opening the door into the suite. Bill followed her. She stopped quickly at the main reception desk. Toni handed her four pink message slips and said good morning. Sara returned the greeting and took a left past the three-dimensional gold metallic sign that proclaimed who they were: Partners Three Advertising. She entered the main work area. Phones were ringing, voices called her name and a group of people at the copier scattered when she flew toward her office. Natalie appeared almost from nowhere. Bill continued to talk as Natalie did — their words mixing together like a Scrabble game. Natalie handed her a cup of coffee as Bill paced and gestured. Sara sat down. She flipped quickly through some stapled sheets of paper on her desk and looked over the ceramic cup at both of them, taking a sip at the same time.

"Should I reschedule this afternoon's meeting?" Bill asked. "It doesn't make us look good, but we'll look worse without any boards to show."

"Bill?" she said in a calm tone.

He continued to talk, barely taking a breath in between sentences. "You see, Sara, that's why I do the scheduling. And Greg should have told me he needed help and then I would've been able to juggle between the two accounts." He was still pacing, one hand scratching the underside of his chin, the other hand gesturing wildly.

"Bill?"

He straightened, turned and was finally quiet. "Yes?"

Natalie dropped her tablet to her side. Her head snapped from left to right as she tried to follow the conversation.

"Why don't you ask Barbara to finish the Dove boards? According to this morning's production schedule, she just finished with the Varsity sketches yesterday." She held the schedule up for him to see. "You know, the one that you put together." She put the schedule back down and, with the end of her pen, flipped to the next page. "I think Barbara's got the time. And she and Jill normally work as a team, so I'm sure she's familiar with the Dove account."

Bill cleared his throat, his eyes closing briefly. "Oh, good idea. Had forgotten about that. I'll get right on it." He spun toward the door, then spun back like a wobbly top. "Good morning, by the way."

Sara smiled. "Good morning, Bill." Her phone rang. "Good morning to you, too, Natalie. Can you get me my appointment schedule for the day?" She reached for the phone.

"Sure. And Paul Brown's waiting to see you." Natalie bit the end of her pencil. "He says it's very important."

Sara laughed. "Of course." She listened intently to the voice on the other end of the line. Derek Edmonds, vice president of communications for Kodak, had received the agency's creative brief, a pitch to market Kodak's new line of cameras.

"There are some really strong ideas here," he said in a flat monotone. "Our second meeting obviously clarified our goals for you, and I'm impressed with the results. I'd like to meet with you again so we can talk more about your proposal."

Sara twirled the phone cord with her finger. "I'm

glad to hear that, Derek. I can fly up next week, if you'd like."

"Yes. That would be fine. During that meeting, I'd also like you to do an agency overview for my staff."

"Not a problem. I'd be delighted."

"Have your secretary check with Claire to see what's open on my calendar."

"Will do, Derek. I look forward to meeting with you again." Sara hung up the phone and leaned back in her chair. If she landed the Kodak account, it would be a huge boost to her career.

"Sara, you have a minute?"

Sara glanced up. It was Paul Brown, her executive vice president of account services. She privately thought of him as her executive pain in the ass. "Paul, how are you this morning?"

Paul smoothed out his gray silk tie. "Couldn't be better. You?"

"Off to a great start. I'm headed to Rochester next week to talk with Kodak again."

Paul sat down in the chair to her left. His dark hair was splashed with gray and the lines around his eyes betrayed his age. "It seems you've got that account pretty well handled. But, other points of view and input may give some more breadth and depth to our proposal."

"Meaning?"

Nervously, Paul rubbed his right earlobe between his fingertips. "Meaning, why don't you let me go to Rochester with you? I've got some ideas that I think will make our position a lot stronger."

"That's great to hear, Paul. Write me a memo outlining them and I'll consider it."

Crossing his legs, Paul leaned back in the chair as

though he intended to stay a while. "We can discuss them over lunch."

"Lunch would be fine." Sara flipped through her Rolodex. "But send me the memo first so I can review what you have in mind. I'm always open to your ideas."

"Are you? Sometimes I wonder."

Sara pulled out the business card she needed and looked up. "As I said, I'm always open to your ideas. That's what we do in this business. Generate ideas. And when it comes to the Kodak account, we need everyone's input — from creative to strategy to marketing."

Paul tugged and evened the sleeves of his crisp, white shirt. "So, you're not going to ride shotgun on this one?"

Sara shook her head and tossed her pen onto the desk. God, he could infuriate her. She would have fired him long ago if he wasn't the CEO's brother-in-law. "Paul, I never ride shotgun on anything. I make the final decisions. But not without seriously considering everything this team puts on the table." Her phone rang again. She ignored it. "We have some of the best people in this business working for us — and I need every one of them right now." She cocked her head to one side. Bill was hovering outside her office again.

Paul grinned. "Well, I'm glad you've taken the time to update me on your managerial philosophy and leadership style. It's good to know what playing field I'm on."

"An even one. The same as everyone else." Sara called over Paul's head, "Bill? You need me again?"

"Yeah, I need to talk about —"

Sara waved him in. "I've got to talk to Bill. Let me have that memo, Paul, and I'll get back to you."

Paul cleared his throat and spoke in a measured tone. "Yes, of course. You'll have it shortly."

Later that morning, sitting at the head of the long conference table, Sara opened the file labeled, "Kodak Account." For the past year she had been working toward this moment — an opportunity to bid on the Kodak camera advertising. If the agency was successful in its bid, it would be the largest account secured in the history of the firm.

Sara looked down the two rows of faces to her left and right. They were all good people — and as anxious to have this victory as she was. "You all know why we're here," she began. "This is a moment we've all worked toward for so many months. The creative concepts are well on their way and the preliminary boards are ready." She indicated the large foam-core boards that hung in the back of the room. "I believe we've begun the development of a unique, refreshing approach to the camera side of Kodak, including concepts for television, print, radio and direct mail." Leaning slightly forward, Sara continued. "I know you realize that we're up against some pretty stiff competition. The top three advertising agencies in the country are breathing right down our necks for this business." Sara held up a recent copy of *Advertising Age*. "These headlines say it all. 'The Top Three Versus the Underdog for Kodak's Twenty Million-Dollar Camera Account.' And then the subhead, 'Will the Underdog Bite?' " Sliding the magazine down the table, Sara said, "Well, I'm here to tell you, the answer is yes. This underdog's going to bite."

The room erupted into cheers and applause.

"The fun starts at the end of next week. I'm on my way to Rochester again at the personal invitation of Mr. Derek Edmonds, vice president of communications for Kodak. He called me this morning."

More cheers and high fives ran up and down the table.

"I've been asked to discuss our creative proposal in detail and do a brief agency overview for Edmond's staff." Sara ran her hands across the cool surface of the table. "Obviously, this is an indication that we're definitely in the running and are being seriously considered."

The room buzzed again with conversation.

"While I'm gone, the creative development work needs to continue. I want all the *I*'s dotted and *t*'s crossed on this one. I expect to return with a date for a formal pitch. Once that's been set, we'll be working nonstop. I want the TV approach we've come up with expanded to include a retail strategy and promotion. Are you with me, Bill?"

"No problem, Sara. I'll get on it right away."

"I also want the radio broadcast redone using the talent we lined up last week. Donna, get them into the studio tomorrow. Make sure you use the revised scripts. Every line needs to be perfect. Shaun will do the final mix and production. Tom can help him if he needs it."

Donna scribbled on her notepad. "The studio's already been booked every day for two weeks just in case."

Sara opened another file. "The direct-mail proposal and comps need more work. All the elements have to be spelled out clearly. It's a unique concept that I don't want falling through the cracks. Jason and Ellen, I'm counting on you to bring it all together, along with the research stats on the direct-TV angle."

Jason nodded. "No problem. We're on top of it."

"As for the print," Sara continued, "it's the best I've ever seen. Let's get it into some focus groups next week to gauge initial consumer reaction. Thank you to Ken and Debbie for their incredible effort. And thanks to all of you for making this happen."

"I'm probably going to join Sara for the trip next week. Bill, you'll have to run a tight ship while we're gone."

Sara let out a heavy sigh before even looking up toward the voice. It was Paul. "We still need to discuss your role, Paul. I believe we spoke about that earlier."

Paul turned in his chair. His six-foot frame made her feel suddenly insignificant. "We did. I just wanted to reinforce the commitment I have to this account and my offer to help you in any way I can. I believe that the two of us, together, can better anticipate and respond to Kodak's concerns and requests. The trip next week is crucial if we're going to earn the opportunity to give a formal pitch."

Sara ignored Paul, determined to remain focused on the group's success as a team. "We'll all play a role in the success of this effort — or its failure. I'll decide who goes with me next week, if anyone. And when we get a date set for the pitch, I'll pick the team for the final presentation." Sara looked over the group, making eye contact with each one of them. "And I can assure each and every one of you, it will be the best team I've ever had the pleasure of putting together for a strategic marketing presentation." Sara gathered her file folders into one neat pile. "Once things are put into motion, those of you who don't go to Rochester need to remember the important role you've played already — and will continue to play with our other clients who still require our services, too. Have a great day. We've got lots of work to do."

The room was hopping with conversation when Sara left. She wondered if the comments were strictly enthusiasm about the Kodak account or talk about her and Paul. The constant friction between them had not gone unnoticed, she was sure. But that friction had to be kept far away from the Kodak account. There was no way she could risk any kind of incident at next Friday's presentation. She wondered what the backlash would be when she told Paul he would not be going with her.

The nightmarish day at the office sent Sara straight to the dance club for a beer. While waiting to place her order, she looked around and nodded in approval. The club, Lavender Nights, was owned by her best friend, Kristie Trevor. Kristie had purchased the property about a year earlier and had invested a large sum of money to make significant improvements. Just off the main entrance, a piano bar had been built where clientele could sit in a quiet atmosphere away from the loud music and dance floor. The dance floor had been enlarged and an outdoor patio constructed adjacent to the main room. "The Patio," as it was called, featured live music by local bands almost every night.

The slender, dark-haired bartender with the wicked grin approached her. "Sara-smile! What brings you out so early this evening?"

"Hard day at work. How are you, Rick?"

"Much better—now that I can gaze into those beautiful blue eyes of yours." He tapped his fingers on the bar, then flipped a cocktail napkin in front of her.

Sara could feel her face redden. "You've got all the lines, don't you, Rick?"

Rick slid open the nearby cooler lid. "Not normally reserved for the ladies. Just for you, my love." He placed the beer in front of her. "I'm absolutely serious, doll. You have the most incredible eyes I've ever seen."

Sara pulled a five from her wallet. "Thank you. That's very sweet. By the way, where's Kris tonight?"

Rick waved off her money. "On the house for you, love. Don't you know? Kristie's out of town until tomorrow."

"No, I didn't know. Or didn't remember."

"She's visiting an old friend."

Sara took a sip of her beer. "I'm glad. That's great for her. She's been working too hard. Too many late nights worrying over these renovations."

"She has, indeed." Rick smiled and patted her

hand. "So, when are you two going to admit you're both crazy about each other — and get married?"

Sara laughed. "You never give up, do you?"

"Not when I see a love match."

"You know we're just friends."

"So you both keep telling me. See ya later, blue eyes. You need anything, just lean over and tap me on the butt."

"I'll be sure to do that."

Rick winked. "Lovely, lovely eyes. Mmm."

Sara watched as Rick waited on a single woman and couple on the other side of the bar. She wondered if he gave her special treatment because of Kristie or because he really liked her. She always had a hard time telling when people were genuine — especially when the compliments were for her.

"He's right, you know."

Sara turned on the hardwood stool toward the voice behind her. "Excuse me?" She was suddenly struck by the features of the woman who now stood next to her. Her shoulder-length dark hair, almost jet black, matched similarly dark eyes. She was tall and lean, formidable, strong. Sara blinked. The resemblance to Joan was undeniable.

"He's right about your eyes. I was almost knocked on my ass when I saw you."

"Well, thank you. That's so nice of you to say."

"Name's Carla. Yours?"

"Sara."

"Ahh . . . a beautiful name, too." Carla sat down and leaned toward her. "It's a damned nice night out."

"Oh, I know. It's perfect weather."

"So, what's a hot-looking woman like you do for a living?"

Sara brushed the hair out of her eyes and looked down at the floor. "I work in advertising. It's quite challenging and I enjoy it very much."

"Yeah? Good. Do refined ladies like yourself dance with strangers?"

"Dance? Oh, certainly. Of course."

"I always lead."

Sara laughed. "I always follow."

"Just what I wanted to hear."

The dance was intimate and charged with the music and the attraction to a familiar stranger. Sara felt instantly warm, flushed. It reminded her of summer, the party, the shadow of Joan suddenly there — looking down at her for the first time almost three years ago. She could almost feel the warm breeze coming off the Chattahoochee River at a park taken over by thirty women in honor of a friend's birthday. She was sitting on the grass in an open area of the park, eyes closed, enjoying the hot sun. The humid August wind blew her hair and cooled the beads of sweat on her forehead. Suddenly, the breeze was gone and she could no longer feel the sun's warmth on her skin. She sensed a presence nearby and opened her eyes to the shadow. The back-lit shadow was tall and haloed. It didn't move.

She shielded her eyes with her hand and squinted. "Excuse me?"

The shadow stooped. The woman had a tanned face, raven hair to the tops of her shoulders, gray eyes the color of dusk. "Sorry. Wanted to introduce myself. I'm Joan, a friend of Carol's."

Sara shook Joan's hand. "So nice to meet you, Joan."

"Carol said you're interested in the volleyball league starting September. I'm coach."

"Oh, how nice. Yes, I thought it would be a good stress-reliever for me. And I really need to get in shape."

Joan smiled broadly. "I'd like to get you on the roster if you're interested."

"That would be wonderful."

"We'll be practicing twice a week at Morehouse. Games are on Saturday. That sound okay to you?"

"Sounds like fun."

Joan called her the following week and asked her to dinner. She arrived at her front door clutching a dozen yellow roses wrapped in green tissue paper. "I know it's our first date, but you're so pretty. And then I saw these flowers . . ." she stammered. "Anyway, here."

"Thank you. They're beautiful. I'll put them in water right away."

Joan sat down in the living room. In the kitchen, Sara called out, "Can I get you something?" She snipped the last quarter-inch of stem from the roses, carefully arranging them one by one into a crystal vase. "I've got an old bottle of wine someone gave me. Some beer. Or, I can make you a mixed drink if you prefer."

"A beer's good. Thanks."

Grabbing a dish towel, Sara twisted the beer cap

off. While pouring it into a frosted mug, she stole a quick look at Joan through the cutaway. She was tall and solidly built. Her dark hair fell just below her shoulders, which were broad and squared. Her face was careworn and heavily lined for someone her age. But there was an attractiveness about her that struck Sara. There was a strange sadness in those smoky eyes, but the face was kind and reassuringly strong.

Carefully, Sara set the vase of roses on the dining room table. "How was your day?"

Joan accepted the beer and shrugged. "It was okay. I'm a firefighter, you know. Today, we cleaned up the engines. We do that when it's slow."

"Oh, well I guess you should take advantage of those slow days when you can."

"Later in the afternoon we got a call. Some kid climbed too far up a tree and we had to get him down."

Sara laughed. "I thought you only rescued cats from trees."

Joan raised her eyebrow and frowned. Slowly, her face broke into a smile. "Oh, yeah. No, we get all kinds of crazy calls. One time I had to crawl into a sewer pipe to get a puppy out. It was all covered in shit, but I made some kid real happy."

"You get to be a hero. That's nice."

Putting her beer down, Joan cracked her knuckles. "It can be. But it's hard when a person's life is at risk. You don't think about it much then."

"No, I guess not."

"So why'd you agree to go out with me?" Joan sat at the edge of the sofa, her arms resting on her thighs. "Nice refined lady like you."

"Refined?"

"Yeah. You know, compared to me." Joan held up her hands. "I get my hands dirty all day. You work in some big office tellin' people what to do."

"Trust me. I get my hands dirty, too."

"Yeah? How?"

"By working with the cutthroats in advertising. It's getting your hands dirty in a different way." Sara crossed her legs and turned slightly toward Joan. "The competition, the bedlam, the constant interruptions and last-minute fires to put out." Sara grinned. "My fires are a little different than yours, of course."

"Yeah, no kiddin'."

"Anyway, people jump from one agency to the next trying to step over anybody and everybody in their way." Sara reached for her beer. "Plus, you've got to wine and dine clients. Really cater to them."

"The big schmooze."

"That's right. Every step of the way. Sometimes it's a bit nauseating."

"Hell, I could never do that." Joan smiled broadly. "Have this bad habit of always sayin' what I think. Probably not a good thing doin' what you're doin'."

"Oh, my heavens, no. Number one rule. Say only what everyone wants to hear."

"Nope, couldn't do it."

"Well, it can be fun though. It's like having a license to lie — because what everyone wants to hear is never what you really want to say, and very rarely ever the truth."

It was Joan's turn to laugh. "Hey, honey. You lost me there."

"Sorry."

Joan had stood and cracked her knuckles again.

"I'm not. I've got a beautiful lady for a date this evening." Offering her hand, Joan helped Sara up. "Let me escort you to dinner."

"Why, thank you."

"Hey, my pleasure. As I'm sure this whole evening will be."

Her first memories of Joan faded away. She was back on the dance floor, in the arms of another woman who was whispering in her ear, "God, you're so damned beautiful. Let's get out of here. Okay?"

Sara answered mechanically, "Okay." Carla took her hand and she followed, stepping in and around the crowd of women. Outside it was warm and the sky was brilliant with stars.

"You hungry at all?" Carla opened the car door for her. "We can go get something quick if you want."

Sara got into a car that smelled like smoke. "No, thanks. I'm just fine."

Back at Carla's, Sara held two glasses while Carla twisted the cork from the wine bottle. The wine went straight to her head. Maybe they should have stopped to get something to eat, she thought. Too late now. She walked slowly around the living room, peering at the flamboyant artwork that covered every wall.

Carla lit a cigarette. "I lived with an artist for two years. These paintings are all that's left of that relationship."

Sara nodded. "It's interesting what remains after two people part ways."

"And what doesn't." Carla took the glass from

Sara's hand. "Some people take a lot more than they leave."

A lump formed in Sara's throat. She thought of Joan and all she had taken — so much more than material possessions. "Yes, that's so true."

A half hour later they were in the bedroom.

"Can you turn a light on?"

Carla grunted, clearly amused. "Most people want all the lights off."

Sara heard the click of a switch. A small lamp softly illuminated the room. No more darkness. She could see the hands that caressed her, the face that leaned toward her lips with a kiss.

Carla ended the kiss quickly and moved down to softly bite her neck. "You're a hot one. Must be my lucky night."

Sara felt her blouse fall open, the straps of her bra pulled away. It had been almost a month. She arched her head back as her nipple slipped into Carla's mouth. She pushed the fear away and let the excitement run through her. Heard herself moan as her hips rose, aching for what had been taken so many times.

"Mmm. I know what you want, baby." Carla tugged anxiously at Sara's jeans. "And I'm the right woman to give it to you."

The hand between her thighs was cold against the heat of her. It found her wetness quickly and lingered there, keeping her on edge.

"Tell me what you want, baby."

"I want you," Sara whispered.

"Tell me what you want me to do to you." With her free hand, Carla squeezed Sara's face between her fingers. "Tell me. I want to hear you say it."

A shiver ran through her when she suddenly remembered what this was. What she was. Calmly, Sara dug her fingers into Carla's shoulders. "The same thing you all want to do to me — and have."

Carla laughed and slapped Sara lightly on the cheek. "What's that, baby?"

Sara looked directly into Carla's coal-black eyes. "Fuck me. Isn't that what you want to do? Fuck me until I come all over you?"

"God, yes. Come all over me, baby, and I'll come too."

Sara moved toward the hand that fucked her and rode the penetration until she thought she might scream. The hand plunged deeper and she opened herself to it, giving what no longer mattered.

"You're incredible," Carla said, barely getting the words out. "Damn, don't make me come first. It'll ruin my reputation."

Sara heard a moan. It wasn't hers. One more reputation ruined, one more thing given in return for nothing. Her own orgasm faded quickly. Even in the light it was dark. She no longer saw the woman next to her and no longer saw herself. But that had been the texture of her life for a very long time.

Clicking on the bathroom light, Sara glanced into the oblong mirror and saw a 35-year-old woman who looked and felt ten years older. Lines of worry and stress ran across her forehead. She noticed a dullness in her eyes — some kind of shadowy film that deepened the blue. She flipped the bangs of her short, blond hair to try to cover the lines above her eyebrows. But some things just couldn't be hidden.

The shower water felt rough instead of soothing. The individual streams of water hit her sore nipples. Lathering the soap all over her shoulders and chest, she moved down to her thighs. Between her legs, a trickle of blood was running all the way from her thigh to her ankle. As she washed herself, she grimaced from the familiar pain.

In bed, she stared up at the ceiling, which was brightly illuminated by the bedside lamp. The swirling textured paint made her dizzy and she closed her eyes to steady herself. Somewhere in the darkness of her mind, she found a restless sleep that instead of dreams brought flashes of the past, rough cuts of three years with Joan. The Joan she loved and the Joan she hated — until she could only hate herself.

Sara stared out the front window. As soon as she saw Joan swing into the driveway, tires squealing, she knew. The driver's side door of the black Honda Passport slammed shut. A familiar stride made its way to the porch. Quickly, Sara darted back into the kitchen to check the meatloaf, still simmering in the oven.

"Hey, what's for dinner?" the sullen voice asked.

Turning slowly, Sara caught Joan's glazed eyes and cocky smirk. "Meatloaf. Your favorite."

"Yeah? Well, I'm hungry. When's it gonna be done?"

"It is done, darling. Sit down and I'll bring it to you. You look so tired."

"Am tired." Joan threw her jacket on the back of a dining room chair. "Didn't you catch the news? Fuckin' two-alarmer in midtown. Some goddamned bakery blew up."

"No, I didn't hear about that." Sara scooped hot biscuits out of a baking pan. "Well, then you need to eat and get some rest."

Dinner was quiet. Sara could feel the mood and prayed for it to end. Maybe Joan would pass out. Maybe, just once, there would be peace.

"I need another beer," Joan growled, shuffling into the kitchen. "You could see the goddamned glass was empty, but will you get up off your ass to get me another? Course not."

Sara followed her. "Joan, why don't you lie down and rest. I'll put the TV on and maybe you'll fall asleep. You look so tired."

Joan swung around and snarled, "Whatsa matter? Don't like my company?"

"You know that's not true." Sara tore a piece of foil and wrapped the leftover meatloaf. "You've had a hard day. I'm just concerned about you."

"Yeah, right. What, you going out tonight or somethin'? Goin' to see your friend, Kristie?" Joan grabbed a can of beer from the refrigerator and slammed the door hard. "That's it, isn't it? That's always it." With one hand, she popped the beer open. "Hate that bitch."

"Joan, please. Don't start. I'm not going anywhere."

"Love to know how many times that bitch has fucked you. You never get enough, do you?"

Sara ignored the rest of the cleanup and walked quickly into the living room. She sank into the section of the sofa next to the fireplace and picked up a magazine.

Joan sat on the other side of the room, her long legs stretched out in front of her. Sara could feel Joan's glare and the hot burning of her own cheeks, which always signaled the descent into the hell of Joan's black mood.

"You gonna just sit there readin' that stupid magazine? I've been workin' all day." Joan gestured toward the kitchen. "The kitchen's still a goddamned mess. You gonna clean it up or what?"

"Later."

"Get over here and talk to me."

Sara lowered the magazine. "I'll talk to you, Joan. I just don't want to fight. Please."

Joan pointed to the spot next to her on the sofa. "I said get over here. Now."

Sara let the magazine slide to the floor. Inside, she could feel herself dying again. She wondered how long it would be before she died once too often and could no longer resurrect herself. She got up and sat down next to Joan. She could smell the beer, sweat and smoke. It was a familiar combination that instantly made her nauseous.

Joan grabbed Sara's shirt collar and jerked her forward until Sara was inches from Joan's face. The kiss was rough. Sara closed her eyes and thought about work. The next day would be busy.

Digging into Sara's arm, Joan got up and pulled. "C'mon. In the bedroom."

Sara resisted, trying to free herself from Joan's grasp. "You're drunk. Not now."

"I said get the hell into the bedroom, slut." Joan gave Sara a hard shove. "If Kristie can fuck you, so can I."

"Joan . . ."

The hand hit her flush across the mouth. "Shut the hell up, for once! Okay?" Joan pushed Sara onto the bed. "All you have to do is lay there. I do all the goddamned work anyway."

The lights went off. Sara held her breath as her clothes were removed. She could hear them landing on the floor across the room. As Joan undressed, Sara suddenly remembered the staff meeting tomorrow at 10:00 a.m. She wondered if Toni had sent the memo out to everyone. She took a conscious breath and imagined herself in the meeting. In her mind, she reconstructed the conference room — the color of the wallpaper, the texture of the carpeting, the tinted windows, the projection screen. She could almost feel the hot cup of coffee that would be within arm's reach. Could almost hear the chatter of voices holding ten different conversations before the meeting began.

With her large hands, Joan pressed her weight down on Sara's arms. "Hey, what're you asleep or somethin'? You dead? Goddamned frigid bitch! Talk to me!"

Sara closed her eyes. The agenda was in her briefcase. It was an important meeting that would cover the agency's top ten clients, strategic positioning for each and goals for the coming year. The agenda was printed on the standard gray paper used by the agency for all its correspondence. Two pages stapled together in the upper left corner.

The hand hit again and her eyes opened.

"Do you want me to fuck you? Huh? Let me hear you beg me."

Two hands grabbed her shoulders and shook them until her jaw popped and neck ached.

"I said beg me, goddamnit. C'mon, be the slut I know you can be."

Her mind fought for that other persona — the one that might save her. The one she kept hidden until moments like this. "So, what are you waiting for?" she asked calmly, seductively. "If you're going to fuck me, then please do. Don't make me wait."

Joan laughed. "That's my girl. My Victorian slut. Always says please. 'Please fuck me, Joan.' So polite."

"Yes, baby. You know that's what I want."

"Yeah, you want it all right." Joan's hands ran roughly across her breasts. "Nice hard nipples now. My prom princess — all nice and wet for me. Call her a slut and she responds — because that's what she is."

The latex penis plunged into her. Somewhere in the distance, it seemed, she could hear Joan grunting like a farm animal just before feeding time. She outlined in her mind what she would say at tomorrow's staff meeting. She thought about each account and where they were in terms of projects and goals: Dove, IBM, UPS, Home Depot, Pepsi and all the others. But then she remembered to pull herself back. Just in time.

"That's it, baby. Fuck me harder. Faster." She clutched Joan's ass and pulled her deeper inside. "I can take all of you — you know I can," she whispered. And just as she felt Joan was about to climax, she faked an orgasm. "Oh, God. Yes. So wonderful. My beautiful lover."

Joan shuddered, moaned and stopped pumping. Sara tried to roll away, but Joan grabbed her by the hair. "Where do you think you're goin', bitch? You're not done yet."

Sara looked up at Joan. "What now, my love?"

Joan knelt on Sara's upper arms, knees pressing hard into Sara's flesh. Sara winced in pain.

"Whatsa matter? Am I hurtin' you?"

"No, darling. I'm fine."

"Good. Now eat me, bitch. I wanna come all over your face."

Sara tugged that persona back — the one she needed, relied on. The person she had almost become. "Oh, baby. You taste so good."

"Goddamned right I do. Yes, make me come, baby. Fuck me with your tongue."

Sara could no longer feel her arms. They were numb and lifeless. She drove her car to work and back, to work and back, to work and back. Seeing every curve, pothole, strip mall, billboard, highway light. Mentally, she drove and drove and drove.

Joan closed her eyes, gritted her teeth and came. She fell over on her side, mumbled a few words and then passed out. Sara turned on the bedside lamp. In her mind, she went over tomorrow's meeting again and again and again. Eventually, she got up from the bed and took a shower. Then she went into the living room, turned on the overhead light and lay down on the sofa. Her body ached, and she knew her face was swollen. But she was too exhausted to get any ice. It had been better than she thought it would be. Tears fell onto her bruised cheeks, the warmth of them pushing her on to sleep.

* * * * *

The "day after," as Sara always referred to it, was always the same. Joan would call her at work every ten minutes. Sometimes, she'd be crying so hard, Sara couldn't understand a word she said.

"I'm sorry, baby. Won't happen again. Don't know what's wrong with me." Sobs and heavy sighs. "The stress at work. It's killing me. I love you so much."

"I love you, too, Joan. But we've got to get some help. I told you about the counseling that's available. We've got to go."

"I know, I know. Make an appointment for next week. I'll go. Promise."

"Okay, Joan. I'll make the appointment."

"Please don't be angry with me. We'll go out tonight, okay? I'll take you to dinner at your favorite restaurant. You'd like that, wouldn't you?"

"Yes, I would. Talk to you later." Sara hung up the phone. She didn't make the counseling appointment, because she had so many times before. And every time Joan had refused to go. Things would be stable for a month or so, and then Joan would snap again. On and on like a repeat nightmare that engulfed her when she least expected it.

Chapter Two

A few days later, Sara and Paul met clients for lunch. Sitting across from Sara, Paul flashed that smirk Sara hated. It always slipped across his face when she was talking to clients or staff and was about to make an important point. The smirk said to her, "You don't know a damned thing and I know everything." He had been a thorn in her side from the very beginning. But he was Richard Sanders' brother-in-law. Sanders was the president and CEO of Sanders International, the holding company that owned Partners Three. When Sara's job became available a year earlier, Sanders had passed Paul over for the promotion. Paul was family, but Sanders' confidence was not high enough to elevate Paul to the top position. Paul resented her and it was not a well-kept secret.

Charlotte Tanner took a sip of lemon water. "So, what you're saying is, our spring campaign will be geared more to younger demographics?"

Sara lay her salad fork on her plate. "Yes. The research we conducted clearly shows that younger kids, ages eight to thirteen, are driving the buying decisions when it comes to your cereal products. Generation Next, they're called. And you should understand that their influence on their parents' buying power is enormous."

Charlotte's partner, Glen Edwards, leaned back in his chair and put his hands in his trouser pockets. "Not like when we were kids and looked into our cereal bowls to find whatever Mom had purchased."

"That's true," Sara agreed. "These young kids aren't afraid to ask for what they want — and many of them are in the store when their parents buy. These are dual-income parents, which makes their access to funds even greater." Spreading out the mock-ups of the new TV ads, Sara pointed out the main sell points. "We've got some really strong visuals here. The commercials are fast-paced and hip for this age group. The writing is short and geared for immediate impact. You need to yell through the TV commercial clutter to get the attention of these kids."

Paul cleared his throat and pushed his plate aside. "Let's not forget that the parent demographics are still important as well. I think our media recommendations are a little off-base. I've brought an adjusted proposal that hits some later evening prime time TV and also includes a print proposal for some middle range demographic magazines." The new proposal was slid toward Charlotte and Glen. "Just some food for thought."

Charlotte picked up the new report. "Sara, is this what you're recommending? I mean does this replace what you've just given us?"

The blood rushed to Sara's cheeks. She was so angry, she felt light-headed. Quickly, she glanced at Paul. He looked totally composed and unconcerned, eating a slice of apple pie. "I haven't had an opportunity to review that material, Charlotte. Do you mind?" Eyes on Charlotte, Sara extended her hand. She forced herself to smile. Charlotte gave her the report. "Why don't I get together with our media people to review all the recommendations? I want to make absolutely certain we're on target here — and I'm sure that we are."

"Do you want this report back, too?" Charlotte asked, still somewhat confused.

"No, you keep that one, Charlotte," Sara responded.

Glen lit a cigar. "You'll call us later, then?"

"Yes," Sara said. "I'm very excited about the new campaign. I know it's going to be a great success for you."

Sara and Paul left the restaurant. Paul merged onto the highway. He hadn't said a word since they said good-bye to Charlotte and Glen. That smirk was still on his face, but he was rubbing his earlobe again.

Sara was furious. "The next time you decide to revise a proposal, I want to know about it in advance. What were you thinking?"

Paul glanced at her, then back to the road. "I honestly thought my numbers, demographics and media selection were more on target. It was only last night that I revised the report. When I saw how off-base the original proposal was, I knew I had to do something."

Sara closed her eyes and took a deep breath. "First of all, the original proposal was not off-base. Secondly, you should have called me at home last night if you had any concerns, or stopped by my office to see me this morning."

Paul shrugged nonchalantly. "Sorry. I didn't finish until late last night. This morning I got tied up with the MCI account."

"Then why didn't you tell me on the way to the meeting?"

"It slipped my mind."

"No excuses, Paul. It's not to happen again. I don't want our clients to think we're not on the same page, strategy-wise. We looked like idiots."

Paul sighed. "Sara, we're never on the same page strategy-wise. And I don't think we look like idiots if we're willing to admit a mistake and offer a correction."

Sara fought for composure. "There was no mistake with the original proposal. The only mistake was the one you made."

"As usual, we're on opposite sides of the fence."

"My intention was to turn this account over to

you, Paul. Just like I've been doing with some other sizable accounts. It's obvious we have trouble working on anything together, but there's got to be some kind of transition period for the client."

"Why don't you let me pick my own accounts?"

"What is it you want?" Sara folded her arms and waited.

"How about Kodak?"

Sara laughed and shook her head. "Of course. Kodak. Well, don't you think it would be wise to get the account first?"

"You mean for you to get the account first."

"That's it." Sara waved him off with her hand. "Discussion over. All of this, everything for the past year, has been nothing but sour grapes and, quite frankly, I'm sick of it."

Paul flipped on the blinker and turned right. "Just make sure I get my plane ticket to Rochester next week."

Sara jerked her head toward him in disbelief. "The discussion's over, Paul. We'll talk about it later," she said between her teeth.

That evening, Sara sat in the last gray, metal chair in the circle. She had stopped home after work and she was late. A woman who was new to the group was talking. She was a small woman with long blond hair that fell straight down to the middle of her back. Her brown eyes, deeply set against China doll skin, nervously darted from person to person. She was hunched over, almost in a crouch, an unlit cigarette fluttering between her fingers.

"This therapist told me we were both batterers. Because I said hurtful things that made Celine hit me. She said that we both needed extensive counseling to get out of the cycle, you know?" The woman lit her cigarette. Her lips trembled. "That's when I figured it was my fault. Just like I always thought."

Dr. Helen Langford, facilitator of the group, spoke in a calm, even voice. "What Karen has experienced is a very serious misconception about lesbian battering. It's called 'mutual battering or abuse.' This misconception is serious because it perpetuates the myth that the partner who is physically abused asked for it. The focus should always be on the immediate issue — that the batterer must stop abusing."

Karen flipped her cigarette ashes into the black plastic ashtray she had propped in one hand. "Celine was happy after that visit to the therapist. She used the whole thing against me and said I was just as much at fault as she was." Meekly, Karen looked at Dr. Langford. "Of course, I believed her. I mean, the therapist is supposed to know, you know?"

Dr. Langford crossed her legs and rested the yellow legal pad on her knee. "Batterers are notorious for using the survivor's self-doubt to their advantage. By labeling Karen as mutually abusive, Celine was avoiding taking responsibility for her own actions." Dr. Langford swung toward her left. "Sara, do you have a comment on this?"

Sara cleared her throat and rubbed her damp palms along her jeans. "Well, a partner may say things that are hurtful. I always tried the opposite tact. I tried placating Joan every step of the way." Sara looked around the room at the women who had experienced the same fear and pain she had. "The point is, your partner has no right to hit you. Not even if you say something hurtful. They have a right to walk away, but not to use physical violence."

"That's correct," Langford said. "The problem with the term 'mutual abuse' is that it really diffuses the issue of responsibility. There's something dangerous and violent going on and the person who's being violent needs to be responsible for her actions."

"I have a kind of similar thing that just happened to me. Sort of weird." Vanessa was the group's rebel. Dressed in ripped jeans and a denim shirt that hung down to her thighs, she sat forward with her elbows resting on the arms of the chair. "You know, these batterers like to control. And I don't mean just when they live with you. They always want control — and they get their kicks that way."

Dr. Langford set the tablet on the floor next to her. "How so, Vanessa?"

"Well, the first abusive relationship I was in was with Pat. Now, we haven't been together for six years. Would you believe she calls me up on the phone last week? A few times a year she calls me, even when I tell her not to." Vanessa threw her hands up in the air. "When I answer the phone, I'm like, now what? She says she called just to say hi because she was having good memories of the two of us. Can you believe that shit?"

Group laughter.

"Then she tells me she's doing great and, by the way, she kicked her new lover out twice because she was acting like I used to."

"How was that?" the doctor asked.

"Yelling at her. Being verbally abusive. And she

says it in this real authoritative tone, you know." Vanessa puffed her chest out. "She says that she hit me and I verbally abused her, so that made it 'even,' quote unquote."

"The main thing we have to remember," Dr. Langford said, "is that lesbians who beat their partners fit the same profile as heterosexuals who batter. They are abusive because they must be in control, and somewhere, at some point in their lives, they were not in control — and still are not in control of their issues and feelings at any given moment. In Vanessa's example, we have a lover who has been gone for six years and still feels the compulsion to call and control."

"Why didn't you just hang up on her?" Kim asked. At only twenty-two, Kim was the youngest member of the group. Her first abusive relationship had begun when she was fifteen. Across her left cheek, she still carried a jagged scar from the knife that almost took her life. A knife that had been held at her throat by her lover of two years.

Vanessa laughed. "Why? She'd just call back. She always does. But if I let her vent and get it out of her system, she won't call for three months."

"Yeah, but once again you let her have control." Kim bit the skin around her fingernails. "That's what they want. Control. Even when they lose their shit."

Sara leaned back in her chair. She was tired. The meeting, while always helpful in reminding her of Joan's refusal to accept responsibility for the abuse she inflicted, left her exhausted and depressed. When Sara thought of the women still out there living the nightmare she lived, it made her physically sick.

After the meeting, Sara knew she should head

straight home and jump into bed. But she missed Kristie so much that she changed her mind. Flipping open her cell phone, she punched in the numbers for the club. Rick answered and told her that Kristie was at home. She drove the two miles through midtown to Grant Park where Kristie lived.

Sara pressed the lighted doorbell.

"Baby doll! Get in here," Kristie said in her thick, Southern drawl.

Sara walked right into a trademark Kristie bear hug. "I missed you."

"Missed you, too."

Sara felt a scratching at her pant leg, heard assorted snorts and snuffles. "Dudley, my one true love! Come up here, boy." Sara lifted Kristie's six-year-old pug into her arms. "Fat boy! And maybe even fatter since I last saw you, but no less handsome!"

"Have you lost your mind? He is not fatter," Kristie said indignantly. "He's still on a diet."

"Yes, of course. The same diet he's been on for two years." Sara patted the dog's stomach. In return, she received a big wet pug kiss. "That's my little man. Best kisser I know!" She put the dog down. He continued to stare up at her, his wrinkled black face tilted, the curled tail bouncing back and forth. Sara took Kristie's hand and walked with her into the living room.

"You look great, baby." Kristie grinned and fumbled for an ashtray on the table behind her. "Been dying to see you."

Sara looked at her friend and quietly

acknowledged what she had always known — that she had loved Kristie since they first met. The bond between them was strong, and Sara had often wondered if they could have made it as a couple. "I'm so glad you're back."

"What do you think of the hair?" Kristie tugged her long, red hair, which was now full of waves and curls.

"It's great. New look?" Sara reached out and ran her fingers through the soft waves.

Kristie shook her head and let the hair fly. "Oh, baby, touch me again!" She put her arms out and turned to each side. "Got to do something to attract the ladies. Not much else is helping!"

"Oh, please. You could have anyone you wanted."

"Honey, do you see them lining up outside the door, begging to come in?" Kristie's dark brown eyes flashed before the grin slipped across her face. "Lord, woman. Ain't no one pounding on my door."

"I am."

"But of course you are. You're the only one I let in!" Kristie laughed hoarsely. "Speaking of attracting women, Rick said he saw you out the other night."

Sara played with the necklace that hung just below her collar. "That snitch. All full of charm but can't keep his mouth shut."

Kristie threw her legs across Sara's lap. "Want something to drink before I get too comfortable?"

"No, thanks. I'm fine."

"I think it's great you went out. Sorry I missed you. I'd have monopolized your time as much as possible."

"Well, I did really just stop by to see you."

"Then who was the lovely lady you left with?" Kristie smiled and winked.

"Wait until I see that Rick. He's going to get a cold beer down his pants."

"Now, now. You know what they say about bartenders, baby. You can tell them all your troubles, but they'll tell everyone else, too." Kristie lit a cigarette. "So, give with the information."

Sara shifted uncomfortably. "Not much to tell."

"Why? What happened?"

"Just a mistake, that's all. My usual poor judgment." Sara turned away. She could feel her cheeks redden with shame.

Kristie took her hand. "If I'm understanding you correctly, you did another Joan thing. Why? You've been doing so well."

"Every once in a while I slip back. Don't know why."

Kristie ran her fingers through Sara's hair and took a long drag on her cigarette. "You still doing the counseling?"

Sara squeezed her friend's hand. "Yes, of course."

"Good. Then everything will be okay."

Sara shook her head. "Sometimes I wonder. Just when I think all the scars have healed and that I might be able to get on with my personal life, I slip into that anger mode — and I don't care what happens."

"It's only been six months, Sara. You've been through hell and back. Don't ask too much of yourself."

"I'm trying. Honest I am."

"And next time your crazy ass gets the urge to go

out, let me know. I'll make sure I'm around." Kristie exhaled a cloud of smoke. "If for no other reason than to throw your ass around the dance floor."

Sara shook her head. "No, no. I can't dance with you."

"What the hell are you talking about?"

"You're a professional."

"Have you lost your mind?"

"Compared to me you are."

Kristie put her cigarette out. "Baby doll, you give me far too much credit." Kristie got up and slid some movies out of the video cabinet. "Hey, I bought a couple of movies for us. Whatcha think? Wanna kick back and watch someone else's drama?"

"Anything would be better than talking about mine."

Kristie plopped back down on the sofa. She pulled Sara toward her and held her close as the first movie started to play. "Now, don't you go falling asleep on me."

Sara laughed. "Oh, brother. Look who's talking. You're the one who always falls asleep."

"Do not."

"Do too."

"Maybe it's because I feel so comfortable with you."

"Maybe."

But not more than ten minutes into the movie, Sara felt her eyes closing. The blackness pulled her under until she found herself running in the rain. It was raining so hard, she could barely see. The water poured down her forehead and into her eyes until she staggered and finally tripped up the steps onto the familiar porch. She pounded her fist against the door — the *boom, boom* of the echo almost drowning out her screams.

Kristie opened the door in her robe. "Oh, God. Baby, what happened?" Kristie grabbed her hands and pulled her inside. "This time I'm gonna kill her."

Sara stood shivering, dripping water onto the carpet. "Just let me stay one night," she called to Kristie, who had left the room. "I'm so sorry. Please."

"Stay one night my ass. You're not going back there. Do you hear me?" Kristie was drying her face with a warm towel. "Godamnit! Look at your beautiful face."

Sara could feel the bruises, sore and pulsating. "I'll be okay. I just have to lie down, Kris. I really need to lie down."

Kristie grabbed her around the waist and led her into the bedroom. "Here, baby. Sit down. It'll be okay."

"I can't."

"Can't what?"

"Sit. I'm . . . hurt." Sara looked at Kristie. There were tears in her friend's eyes. It was the first time she'd ever seen Kristie cry. "It's not that bad. I'll live."

Kristie put one arm around Sara's back and the other beneath her legs. Lifting her gently, she laid her on the bed. Her shoes came off. Her wet jacket. The rest of her soaked clothing. A shiver went through her. Then she felt the nightshirt go over her head. All the time, Kristie whispered, "It's okay, baby. It's okay. You're safe now." One arm through a sleeve, then the other. "It's okay, Sara. No one's going to hurt you again."

The warmth of the waterbed felt good against her bruised skin. Kristie pulled the covers up.

"You get some rest now. Sure you don't need to see a doctor?"

"No. Honest. I'm okay."

"I'll be right outside the door if you need me."

"Don't leave me alone. Please."

Kristie sat down on the edge of the bed and rubbed her hand lightly through Sara's hair. "Whatever you want, you got it."

"Hold me?"

Kristie turned off the light.

"Can you leave the light on? I can't sleep in the dark."

"No problem. I'll leave the bathroom light on and crack the door. How's that?"

"Thanks."

Kristie took Sara into her arms. Sara winced and sighed. Her entire body ached and throbbed.

Kristie jumped. "Did I hurt you?"

"No." Sara patted Kristie's arm. "It's just that everything hurts. Inside and out."

"I'm sorry, baby." Kristie kissed her forehead. "You know you can't go back there — no matter what Joan says, does, threatens. You can't."

"No, I can't."

"Besides, I'm gonna kill the bitch anyway."

"Shh. She can't hurt me anymore." Sara felt the tears come. And when they started, she couldn't stop them. "I finally figured this out, Kris."

"What?"

"That it's not my fault. That she needs help. And

I can't be the one to help her." Sara wiped tears from her eyes. "She has too much anger toward me. I don't know why, but I can't make it go away. I thought I could, you know. That I could fix everything for her. That I could be the perfect partner."

"You're right, honey. It's her, not you."

"The counseling has helped. I should have gone long ago."

"You were trying to make things work. There's nothing wrong with that."

"I've become close to this group. We've all been struggling through the same thing. And now I know what they all know." Sara laid her head on Kristie's shoulder. "That Joan's not going to change. And that I need to put myself first."

"Stop being the victim?"

"Yes. When you love someone it's so hard to see. You hope things will get better. But they never do."

"You can stay here as long as you need to."

Sara woke up from the dream and gasped for breath. Her chest heaved and she broke into a sweat. Finally, she remembered she was in Kristie's living room and that the rain-soaked dream was a flashback she had lived over and over again.

"It's okay, baby. It's okay." She felt two strong arms wrap themselves around her.

"I'm sorry. Was I dreaming?"

"Yes. It's okay. You're safe. Remember?"

"I remember everything but the movie."

Kristie chuckled. "That's okay. I fell asleep, too."

"Are we getting old, do you think?"

"No, I think I'm fucking boring."

"Don't be ridiculous."

"It's true. Stick with me, kid. You'll get rest if nothing else."

"No, I always get a lot more than that."

Kristie kissed Sara's forehead. "So do I."

On Saturday morning, Sara made a quick call to Delta. She needed to get on a plane that afternoon. The call from her brother had come without warning.

"Mom's in the hospital again," Rod said. "You better come home."

Her mother had many health problems over her lifetime, including diabetes and high blood pressure. The diabetes had done the most damage, primarily to her mother's eyes and kidneys. Two years ago, one kidney had completely failed. Fighting diabetic blindness and living with one kidney was finally taking its toll.

"They think she got the pneumonia during this last hospital stay," her brother had said. "She's on a ventilator, Sara. I don't like the feeling I'm getting."

"I'll be home as soon as I can."

She had spoken to her mother every day for the last three weeks while she had been in and out of the hospital. Over and over again, she had asked her mother if she wanted her to come home.

"Don't you dare fly all the way up here," she had said in that authoritative tone only a mother could manage. "I'm fine. They just need to adjust my medication. Once they patch me up, I'll be home again and then back to work. Don't worry."

Worry had long since overtaken her thoughts and fears. In the visitor's lounge of the hospital's Intensive Care Unit she had a sudden, uncontrollable urge for a cigarette. She hadn't smoked in ten years. Waiting impatiently for visiting hours to begin, she closed her eyes and clutched the arms of the chair. Ten minutes seemed like ten hours.

Sara pressed the large silver button on the wall. The doors in front of her automatically swung open into the ICU center. The nurse's desk was immediately in front of her. A nurse was chattering on the phone while a doctor scribbled notes onto a clipboard. She waited self-consciously while the nurse finished the phone call.

"Can I help you?"

"Elizabeth Gray's room, please."

"Are you family?"

"Her daughter."

The whoosh of the ventilator startled her. It was a large machine that hissed air through a tube into her mother's lungs. Her mother lay motionless, eyes closed, a white sheet covering her up to the waist. The hospital gown bared her arms, which lay at each side. They were bruised from shoulder to wrist from the constant sticks of the blood lab technicians. Another machine hummed and beeped as it dripped an array of drugs into her mother's body.

Sara slid in between the tubes and machines to get closer. She stroked her mother's arm lovingly. "Mom. It's Sara."

The familiar hazel eyes opened. Her mother appeared startled and her face twitched with excitement. Tears pooled in her eyes as she struggled to speak. But the tube in her throat choked off the words. She reached out and grabbed Sara's hand.

"It's okay, Mom. I'm only here because I couldn't stand to be away from you anymore."

Still clutching her hand, her mother gestured toward the table at the end of the bed. Sara saw the tablet and pen and immediately understood. She gave the pen to her mother and held onto the tablet, supporting it for the unsteady fingers that struggled to write. Sara read the words to herself. "Please don't leave me."

"I'm not going anywhere. Everything's fine. You're going to be okay."

Her mother shook her head.

"It's true, Mom. That's what the doctors tell us. You're breathing mostly on your own now. Pretty soon they'll have this tube out and you'll be back on your feet again."

Her mother shook her head again and scribbled on the tablet. "Blood clot on lung?"

"No blood clot. Pneumonia. But you've beaten it. You're going to go home soon."

"Never going home again."

"Yes, you are. I promise."

"How's Daddy?"

"Fine. Getting lots of attention, so don't worry about him. You just concentrate on resting and getting better."

For the next three hours she sat at the end of the bed and watched her mother sleep. Occasionally, a nurse would come in and chitchat while checking the machines and refilling the drips. Line after line dripping drugs with names too long for her to pronounce. For an instant, she allowed herself to think about what it would be like to lose her mother — and in that instant she felt the most intense pain she had ever known. Like her friend, Kristie, her mom had been a constant source of strength, the calm voice on the phone, a lifeline to family and what used to be home. There were times they disagreed, argued, hurt each another. But during the last ten years, they had grown steadily closer until the ever-present bond of mother and daughter became the glue that held them together. Sara glanced up and made herself see the changes. Her mother's face was ashen. There was an unfamiliar fragility masking the strength that had been this woman. She looked tired. Beaten. Panic suddenly ran through her. But she turned away from it. Her mother was not going to die. The doctors had said she was improving. It would take time, but her mother would be well again. She imagined her mother sitting in her favorite living room chair, laughing at some story Sara told her about life in the big city. About her crazy job and the people she'd met. That's what Sara held onto — the sound of her mother's laughter drowning out the machines in that cold, impersonal hospital room. Sara got up and held her mother's hand, crying softly while her mother slept.

Chapter Three

In 1879, London was the center of the photographic and business world — and London is where George Eastman went to obtain a patent on his plate-coating machine. An American patent was granted the following year. On January 1, 1881, the Eastman Dry Plate Company was formed in Rochester, New York. In 1883, Eastman startled the photography trade with the announcement of film in rolls. With the development of the Kodak camera in 1888, he laid the foundation for making photography available to everyone.

The first Kodak camera was pre-loaded with enough film for 100 exposures. It could be easily carried and handheld during operation and was priced at $25. After exposure, the whole camera was returned to Rochester, where the film was developed, prints were made and new film was inserted—all for $10.

Sara stood in the lobby of Kodak's corporate headquarters reading the history of the company etched on the wall in front of her. The next two hours would be critical to her success at Partners Three Advertising. She felt quietly confident—even calm. There was an inner conviction that her staff would do their best while she was gone, and nothing less. This morning, she would do her best as well. She would not let them down.

Paul Brown had been furious when she told him that he would not be accompanying her to Rochester. The discussion was heated, but Sara held firm. She was not willing to run the risk of an open confrontation with Paul during today's meeting with Kodak. The effect could be disastrous.

He'd leaned his lanky frame against the doorjamb. "You're making a big mistake, Sara."

"I don't think so. I'm going to Rochester to attempt to set up a formal meeting so we can present our strategy, ideas and creative concepts." Sara packed some files into her briefcase. "It's what we've all been working toward. Once that meeting is set, I'll need everyone, including you, to work their butts off day and night."

"What if you don't get a meeting?" Paul folded his arms across his chest and smirked. "I'm sure the home office will be very interested if that happens."

"I'll get one." Sara walked in front of her desk and sat on its edge. In an almost pleading tone, she said, "Paul, I need you here to motivate staff and get things in shape for the pitch. I need you to review everything thoroughly while I'm gone. I'll be back on Monday and we need to be ready to roll. Your presence here is very important."

Paul shook his head back and forth, tugging at his earlobe — a habit that was beginning to drive Sara to distraction. "I never thought you'd be the type."

"Excuse me?"

"To sacrifice the good of everyone for your own career goals. To make certain you get all the credit."

Sara stood up straight. Her left eyelid twitched — a sign of anger. "The credit for any success we may achieve with Kodak, Paul, will go to everyone who works at Partners Three. That's been a mainstay philosophy of mine ever since I got here — to make sure everyone gets the proper credit and recognition for their talents and efforts. You know that's true and I can't believe you would say otherwise."

Paul shrugged nonchalantly. "I call it as I see it right now. It doesn't please me to say it any more than it pleases you to hear it."

"Well, I can tell you right now that I'm not pleased. We need to talk when I get back, Paul. And we will."

Paul had turned sideways to leave. "I have no problem with that. Just let me know when you return."

Sara tried to shove the run-in with Paul out of her mind. She had more important things to think about.

"Sara, how are you?"

Sara turned away from the wall that footnoted the history of one of America's oldest and most beloved companies. Taken completely off guard, she gasped audibly, a sound that seemed to echo throughout the expansive lobby.

"I'm sorry, Sara. I know this is a surprise. But, my decision to be here was made at the last minute."

Sara felt an incredible urge to pinch herself to see if she was really awake. "Richard, how wonderful to see you. I'm so sorry, but you did startle me."

Richard Sanders, president and CEO of Sanders International, holding company of Partners Three, thrust out his hand to shake hers. "Again, I apologize. It's been so long. How are you?"

"Well, very well. And you?"

"Couldn't be better." Sanders buttoned his expensive navy blue suit coat. "Let me reassure you about why I'm here. First of all, I wanted to congratulate you on the success you've had so far with Kodak. Needless to say, I'm impressed. Kodak entertains very few account management proposals. To have gained their interest is extremely remarkable."

"Thank you, Richard."

"Secondly, I thought it might be beneficial to let Kodak know that Partners Three is backed by a large organization dedicated to serving them. I'd hoped you wouldn't mind, despite the lack of notice, if I represented our national and international presence to them."

Sara's mind raced. Why was he really here? Why would he fly all the way from San Francisco at the last minute? "Of course not, Richard. I think the agency's roots are important for Kodak to know."

"Then my presence won't interfere with your presentation?"

"Not at all."

Derek Edmonds, vice president of Kodak's communications department, and three of his top communications staff people sat on one side of the solid wood conference table. Sara and Richard faced them. It felt like a face-off, Sara thought. But she had plans to change that. Sara introduced herself again — and introduced her boss. "It's an honor to speak with you today," she said. "When I'm finished, I hope you'll have a better understanding of what our agency is all about and the strong commitment we have to every one of our clients, large and small."

Sara began her presentation with an introductory talk about Partners Three and who they were in the advertising industry.

"Our job is to increase the power of your communications through a complete range of integrated marketing services," Sara said, smiling and making eye contact with each member of the group. "Partners Three coordinates every comprehensive communications effort with the goal of balancing the synergy that helps each message, in whatever medium, to work harder."

Getting up, Sara clicked to the next PowerPoint slide. "We base each creative message on a solid strategy to convey a consistent image. This pyramid shows how that's done. Through superior execution, creative consistency and strategic planning." Sara clicked to the next slide. "Partners Three is not just an advertising agency in the traditional sense. While we provide full agency services, we operate differently behind the scenes. Our agency is comprised of seasoned experts who have spent years learning their art and craft. These experts are the same people who will work with you directly every day, overseeing each aspect of the Kodak account."

Sara talked for another ten minutes. As she walked up and down Kodak's side of the conference room table, she outlined the agency's present client base and the campaign successes that had brought them many awards and much national notice. She finished by turning the talk over to Richard. He spoke eloquently about the holding company's international status and the impact it would have on Kodak's future success in the consumer camera market.

Sara then fielded questions from Kodak's staff. Calmly, she answered questions about aging baby boomers, demographics and disposable income, creative strategy and overseas competition. When the meeting was concluded, Derek Edmonds asked to speak with Sara and Richard privately.

Edmonds' office was plush, with a wet bar, brown leather furniture and expensive artwork on every wall. Mementos of his many years with Kodak lined the shelves — corporate citizenship awards, recognition plaques, token gifts from the company. Sitting down in his desk chair, Edmonds looked up and smiled pleasantly. He appeared to be in his middle fifties.

His blond hair and green eyes accentuated his rugged good looks. Broad shoulders filled out his stocky frame.

"I was surprised and pleased to see you here, Mr. Sanders. I've heard a great deal about your firm."

"Please. Richard is fine." He leaned back in his chair. "It's exciting to be here. Obviously, the Kodak business is very important to us, far beyond any monetary issues."

"That's good to know. Thank you." With a nod to his right, Edmonds indicated Sara. "Sara has impressed me greatly. We don't consider very many agency proposals, but as soon as we met I was immediately interested in what you have to offer."

Sara slid her briefcase to the floor. "I've enjoyed our talks, Derek. And the opportunity to be here again."

Edmonds pushed some papers out of his way. He leaned slightly forward and folded his hands. "What I'd like to do is set up a time for a full-blown creative presentation by your staff, Sara. Can you be ready by the end of July?"

Sara quickly calculated the time in her head. It was a little over three months. More than enough time to nail down a comprehensive strategic recommendation. "Yes, of course. No problem."

"Good. I'll have my secretary call you with an exact date. Our objective is to get all of the agencies to present within a two-week time frame."

"That sounds great. We're very excited about this opportunity, Derek. I can assure you that you won't be disappointed in the results."

"I'm sure I won't. I look forward to seeing you

again in July. If you need anything in the meantime, just let me know. I'll have my secretary show you out."

Later that evening, Sara lay on her bed in the hotel room watching a pay-for-TV movie. The excitement of her success made her restless. Everything had gone as planned, despite the surprise appearance by Richard Sanders. His last-minute arrival still puzzled her. She also felt the intense pressure of the work that lay ahead. She had come to Rochester with only one objective in mind — and that objective had been achieved. Tomorrow the long road back to Rochester would start all over again. Unable to focus on the movie, she decided to go out.

The doorman hailed her a cab and she gave the cabdriver the address of a late-night club she remembered was located downtown. She had been to Rochester many times to visit an old college friend who had since moved to Arizona. She wondered if the club was still there.

As they rounded the corner onto Blair Street, she saw the familiar neon lights of the building at the end of the block. Inside, the bar hadn't changed much. It was more of a lounge atmosphere, with a dance floor in a separate room in the back. The main room looked like someone's living room with coffee tables and armchairs, sofas and TVs. There was a traditional bar to her right and that's where she sat. She waved the bartender down and ordered a beer.

Looking around, she saw groups of women talking and laughing, playing pool, drinking, watching TV. The club actually reminded her of a popular lesbian bar in Atlanta. It had been a favorite place, and she and Joan had gone there frequently.

One night, she had suffered silently as Joan held another woman on her lap. Joan was slightly drunk and the other woman's girlfriend was not at all happy. Sensing trouble, Sara took Joan by the hand and asked her to dance. Joan jerked her hand away and continued flirting. Finally, Joan announced that she and her new lap-mate, Tammie, were going to play pool. Sara and Tammie's girlfriend, Barbara, flashed each other a can-you-believe-this look. Not knowing what else to do, they grabbed their drinks and followed Joan and Tammie to the pool table.

Joan was in one of those please-pay-attention-to-how-wonderful-I-am moods that Sara hated. Loud and obnoxious, she was showing off.

"Damn, don't you people know how to play? Let an expert show you!" Joan pulled a cue from the rack and rolled it across the surface of the pool table. "This one'll do." At the edge of the table, Joan leaned over Tammie's back and instructed her on the finer points of lining up a shot. "Listen, baby. All you got to do is look down the long shaft of the cue and aim. Give it a try."

Tammie brought the stick back and hit the ball solidly. It banked off the rim and headed straight for the corner pocket, but missed. Tammie gave Joan a coy smile. "Sorry. I tried."

Joan put her hand at the back of Tammie's neck

and squeezed. "No problem, sweetie. Just remember, a slow, easy stroke is better. It's like making love. Or at least that's how I do it."

Tammie giggled and stepped away from the table. She stumbled right into Joan's waiting arms. "Oops. Why, excuse me."

"Not to worry. I gotcha covered, honey."

While the other team attempted their shot, Joan made a nuisance of herself. She put her leg up on the table, shoved her hand inside the pocket they were aiming for and got the attention she craved. Sara couldn't take anymore and left the room. Wandering outside, she stood against the railing of the zigzag cement walkway bordering the upper floor of the complex. The skyline of Atlanta was in perfect view, cutting the horizon with glittering lights and angled shapes that seemed God-like to her. Cool air blew through the breezeway on a night that was clear and oddly quiet. A sense of peace came over her, but she didn't know why. For the first thirty-two years of her life, she had lived in Pennsylvania — a small-city girl who loved the mountains and lakes and fiery Northeast autumns. But there was a restlessness in her soul and an apprehension in her heart that told her she was missing something important. So she decided to move and start her life over again. Atlanta seemed like the perfect place. The city was booming with jobs and the Centennial Olympic Games had revitalized its image.

So much had happened since she arrived in Atlanta, she found herself wondering if she had made a huge mistake. In light of all her personal turmoil, she thought she should hate this city — its horrible traffic, crowded restaurants, rainy winters, hot summers and sometimes flagrant anti-North sentiment. Every time she saw the Georgia state flag with its inflammatory stars and bars, she inwardly cringed. But for some strange reason, she could not hate Atlanta. At least not the beauty of it. Its massiveness seemed oddly contained and orderly, unlike New York City, where chaos, as deeply as it cut into that city, went unnoticed for the sheer commonality of it. The crisp shadows of steel that rose from the Atlanta skyline were comforting because they were unchaotic and, in that sense, nothing like her life. Her life no longer knew order. The unexpected seemed to ambush her at every step.

"What the hell are you doing out here?" Joan grabbed her arm and pulled her from the rail.

"Admiring the view. It's such a beautiful night." Sara took Joan's hand. "Look. Isn't it incredible?"

"Yeah, yeah. It's real nice." Joan cocked her head in the direction of the bar. "Come back inside, okay?"

"All right."

Joan stared off toward the view. "Look, I realize I was being an idiot. I apologized to Tammie and her girlfriend. Now I'd like to apologize to you. I'm sorry."

This was the Joan that had always surprised her. The Joan she'd seen so infrequently and loved so much. "Don't worry about it. How about asking me to dance?"

"My pleasure."

The bartender snapped, " 'Nother beer for you?"

Sara was jolted back to the present. "Yes, thank you."

"You from out of town?" A tall woman with wire-framed glasses was standing behind Sara, one arm leaning toward the bar for a wave at the bartender. "Hard to get a drink here sometimes," she said, smiling.

"It's crowded tonight," Sara agreed. When the female bartender clunked the beer down on the counter, Sara said, "You've got another customer right here."

The bartender took the woman's drink order.

"Hey, thanks for the help. Appreciate it. By the way, you never answered my question. You from out of town?"

"Yes. How did you know?"

The woman laughed hoarsely. "Well, for one thing, I've never seen you in here before. And since this is the only women's bar within a fifty-mile radius, you get to know the regulars pretty well."

"Makes perfect sense."

"Plus, you look more like big city to me."

"Rochester's a big city."

"Yeah, sure it is. But I mean like metropolitan big city. You know, like New York, Chicago, L.A."

"I'm from none of those."

The woman scratched her head. "Hmm. Guess I was wrong, then. You're probably from some little farm town in Vermont or something."

Sara chuckled. "No, I'm no farm girl. Atlanta."

"Ahh, one of those Southern belles."

"Oh, my heavens. Not by a long shot. I'm a northern transplant like everyone else who lives down there."

"You doing anything tonight? I mean, I guess you're here on business or something. But I could show you around the city, if you like."

Sara was about to answer when a fight erupted on the other side of the bar.

The woman standing next to her craned her neck to see what was going on. "Uh oh. I smell trouble."

Two women were toe to toe, screaming at each another. There was a sickening crack. Sara flinched. One of the women had slapped the other flush across the cheek. Suddenly, Sara got up. Looking at the stranger standing next to her, she was flooded by flashbacks. She grabbed her coat and left the bar, hurrying down the street as fast as she could.

"Hey, hey!"

She heard the woman's voice behind her. Breaking into a run, she ignored her and didn't look back.

"Hey, what'd I say? I'm sorry."

The woman's footsteps faded. Sara continued to run.

On her way back to Atlanta from Rochester, Sara scheduled a lay-over in Pennsylvania. It would give her another opportunity to visit her mother, who was still in the hospital.

Her mother sat on the hospital recliner picking at her lunch. Just as the doctors predicted, she had beaten the pneumonia and was finally removed from the ventilator. Sara wasn't at all sorry when they came to take the machine away.

"I'm so happy to see you," her mother said, patting her lightly on the arm. "But it's so expensive for you to be flying here all the time."

"Mom, please don't worry about that. I flew in on

my way back from Rochester. The important thing is that I'm here with you."

Her mom pushed the tray of food away. She'd hardly eaten anything. There was a fatigue in her eyes Sara had never noticed before. It frightened her.

"I had a long talk with the doctor today, Sara."

Sara stiffened, trying to mentally prepare for any bad news. "Oh? What did he say?"

Although there was little eye contact, her mother was very matter-of-fact. "I asked him, all things considered, how much time I had."

Sara's fingers dug into the vinyl chair. "And he said?"

Her mother shrugged. "Oh, about six months. That's how long he thinks my kidney will last, since the second one decided to quit on me."

Taking a deep breath, Sara fought for composure. "How do you feel about that?"

Looking directly at her, her mother spoke in a calm almost-whispered tone. "I'm at peace, Sara. I've done all that I wanted to do and more. I've raised four wonderful children, served my community and worked hard to improve the lives of others." Her mother paused, deep in thought. "We all have to face the inevitable, Sara. If it's my time, then I need to be ready. And you need to be ready, too."

Sara could no longer hold back the tears. "But, Mom, you're such a big part of my world. I can't imagine my life without you."

Leaning back in the olive-green hospital recliner, her mother rested her hand beneath her chin. "I have three fine sons. Three wonderful daughters-in-law. Seven grandchildren who have brought me great joy." Her eyes closed as if to catch the glimpse of a memory. "And while I'll miss every one of them very much, you're the person I'll miss most of all, Sara." The eyes opened again and one tear fell, and then another.

Together, they sat and cried quietly until her mother fell asleep.

Chapter Four

The late-April sun was hot. Piedmont Park was packed with people playing Frisbee, softball, jogging, walking their dogs, having picnics. And that was what Kristie had planned—an afternoon picnic with friends. Some of the women Sara had already met, but several of them were new to Kristie's entourage. Kristie introduced everyone, and they picked a spot that was nicely shaded.

Kristie put her arm around Sara's shoulder. "How's your mom doing?"

"Holding steady. I don't think I'm handling it very well, and I think she expects me to be strong."

"Be what she needs you to be when you're there with her. When you're here with friends, you don't have to be strong. You can just be you."

"Do you know what she said to me?"

"What?"

" 'I expect you to be levelheaded.' My mother's dying and she wants me to be levelheaded."

"She wants your strength."

"You're right, of course. I just hope I have it to give." Sara turned away from Kristie and staved off the panic concerning her mother. "Dudley, what are you doing?"

The small pug was face-first into one of the coolers.

"You little monster. Trying to sneak a hot dog before it's even cooked!" Sara grabbed the pug and secured his leash to the nearby tree. He snorted indignantly, his tongue hanging sideways from his mouth. "I know, I know. But you'll just have to stay here until we're done eating." She patted him on the head and kissed his velvety black ears. "And I'll be sure to save you a hot dog, diet or no," she whispered. She turned around and put some more drinks into the large blue plastic cooler. "What's on the menu, besides hot dogs, Kris? I shoved just about every kind of soda and juice in here I could possibly think of."

"I can always count on you." Kristie peered into the other cooler. "Yes, we've still got weenies to roast, despite Dudley's attempt to run off with them. And hamburgers to cook, potato salad, pasta salad, chips and pretzels and some other assorted goodies." Attaching the metal legs to the portable hibachi, Kristie found a level piece of ground to hold it steady. With a swagger back toward the cooler she said, "Now the famous meat chef must get cooking."

Jennifer, one of the bartenders employed at Kristie's nightclub, helped Sara lay out two large blankets. "Great day for a picnic, ain't it?" The short, thin woman bounced around the blankets, smoothing them out until they were perfect.

"Oh, it's just beautiful."

Jennifer stood with her hands on her hips, squinting into the sun. "You ain't been in the club much lately. How come?"

Sara sat down on the edge of the quilted blanket. "If I know Kris is going to be there, I'll stop by to say hello. But mostly I go home after work and read or watch TV."

Jennifer looked surprised. "Don't you go out on the weekends — a pretty lady like yourself?"

"I used to. Not much anymore."

"You ain't dating nobody?"

Sara smiled sheepishly. "No. Really not interested right now."

Shaking her head, Jennifer knelt down and sat with her legs folded underneath her. Her long brown hair blew across her face. "Man, how do you do that? If I don't have a date at least once a week, I go nuts."

"Well, I never really dated, to tell you the truth. Not in the true sense of the word. If I met someone and went out with her, it always turned into a relationship right away. I don't want that anymore."

Jennifer pointed at her and nodded. "That's the

problem, ya see. Lesbians don't know how to date. Ain't that right, Kris?"

Kristie waved smoke from the grill. "What?"

"Ain't it right that lesbians don't know what the word *date* means?"

Flipping a hamburger, Kristie laughed. "Baby, no lesbian knows what that word means. A first date is what happens the day before you move in."

Overhearing the conversation, several of the other women laughed.

Jasmin Matthews, a short, attractive black woman Sara had never met, said, "Girl, I asked this woman out one time — and she had a ring for me the next day." Everyone groaned. "I'm not lying. Now I know I'm interesting and charming, but really!"

"Some of these hot dogs are done!" Kristie pushed the cooked meat to the side of the grill. "Ladies, not only does a date mean instant marriage in the lesbian community, but . . . when you're dating someone, it's automatically assumed that you're fucking them. I don't quite get that."

Jennifer howled. "Well, aren't you?"

"Damn you, Jen. Come a little closer and I'll skewer you. No! Why does a date mean you go to bed? What about getting to know someone or, now hang onto your pants, why not date a few women at a time?"

"Yeah, right. That'll never happen." Susan, Kristie's promotions coordinator, helped herself to a hot dog. "Simultaneous dating will never happen in our community. It's just not accepted. You date one woman at a time, you sleep with them somewhere along the line and then you call U-Haul."

Lots of laughter.

"That's how we all get caught in what I like to call the two-year date syndrome." Kristie reached for the ketchup. "You meet someone, move in, and it lasts for two years 'cause you never took the time to get to know 'em, never really did know 'em, you end up knowing 'em and wonderin' who the hell they are. By that time two years are up. So, it's been a two-year date."

"Man, I can barely handle a date for one night," Jennifer said, flopping over onto her side. "But Kris is right. Some of these women you meet call and bug you after one date, and if you don't end up being stalked, it's a freakin' miracle. There ain't no such thing as friendly dating, either. If it's not serious right away, it can get downright ugly."

Sara cleared her throat. "Well, if I may make a comment, I'd like to say that honesty is also an issue."

"What do you mean, babe?" Kristie plopped down next to her and leaned against her shoulder.

"Well, it's okay with me, really, if it's going to be a one-night stand and I know it. I mean, if it's what both parties agree to. What I have a problem with is when other women play you."

Jennifer grunted. "I know just what she's gonna say."

"Yes, you're made to feel like you're that special person she's always wanted in her life. Emotionally, she manipulates you into thinking that there's a commitment—or at least an honest direction toward one. Then you find out she has a hidden agenda, or she just wanted a few months of fun in and out of bed."

"What do you mean by hidden agenda?" Susan

asked. “I understand the playing scenario. But give me an example of the hidden agenda one.”

Sara leaned back on her hands. “Well I had a friend once who really fell in love. The woman she was seeing was quite charming. A real pro at the playing game, if you know what I mean. She was always telling my friend how pretty she was, how much she loved her laughter and her company. She really built up her self-esteem, made her feel beautiful when she hadn’t felt that way in such a long time. My friend ended up getting dumped, of course. Didn’t mean a damned thing to that woman. It was all just a game to her.” Sara bit her lower lip. “My friend really got hurt. I don’t think she’s ever gotten over it.”

“That sucks,” Susan said, reaching for a soda.

Kristie bit into a hot dog. “Crap like that happens every damned day. You just want to smack the dog-shit out of people anymore.”

Sara raised her eyebrows at Kristie.

Swallowing a bite of her hot dog, Kristie said, “I’m sorry, baby.” She leaned over and kissed Sara’s cheek. “Shouldn’t have said that. Just a figure of speech.”

Sara shrugged and grabbed Kristie’s hot dog. She took a big bite out of it and said, “Mmm, this is good. Bet Dudley would like the rest of this.”

“Hey,” Kristie said, lunging toward Sara. “Give that back.”

Sara shoved the hot dog into Kristie’s open mouth. Mustard ended up on the end of her nose. The entire group roared with laughter.

“Nothing like the wrath of a woman,” Susan commented.

"Damn, ain't that the truth?" Kristie said, holding what was left of the hot dog. "Women. Ya can't live with 'em, can't live without 'em."

"Well, on that note I think some fun is in order!" Jennifer said, bouncing up from the ground. "Who's up for kite-flying? I've got some beauties in my car!"

Kristie smiled broadly. "Hell, Jen, you always got beauties in your car. Tell us something we don't know."

"Very funny. Be right back."

About ten minutes later, Sara watched as the multi-colored box kite floated high above her. Susan had hold of another one that looked like the wings of a large bird, dipping and soaring, struggling to break free. There was a part of her that wanted to be up there, too, gliding along on air not bound to anything.

"How long have you known Kristie?"

Jasmin sat down next to her and rested her forearms on her thighs.

"Two years. We've been best friends."

Jasmin's hair was short curls and dark, her eyes an ice-melting brown. Her skin was brown-black, like the chestnuts that fell from the tree in Sara's backyard. Sara found her extremely attractive.

"I met her at a Youth Pride fund-raiser a few months ago. She's a great person."

"Yes, she is," Sara agreed.

"I'm the executive director of the Atlanta Community Food Bank." Jasmin stretched her legs across the blanket and leaned against the pine tree. "Ever heard of it?"

"Oh, of course. My company's done food drives for your organization. Around the holidays, I believe."

"Good! I'm glad to hear that."

Sara lay down on her back, shading her eyes from the sun with her hand. "It's quite a large food bank, I've heard."

"It is," Jasmin said. It was hard not to notice the pride in her voice. "We've got over seventy thousand square feet of storage, plus another seventy-five thousand cubic feet of walk-in refrigeration and freezer space. We've also got a small fleet of vehicles that goes out to pick up the food donated by companies like yours."

Sara said, "You must help feed a lot of people."

Jasmin was running her hand through the already plush green grass. "We help to furnish all or part of about a million and a half meals per month that are served by agencies, shelters, soup kitchens, orphanages, halfway houses and nursing homes. We also help supply emergency food pantries, which distribute food to about seven hundred and fifty thousand people each month. About half the people we feed are kids."

"That's wonderful. I can tell you really love your work. What a great feeling to know that you're helping all those children — and others who need it."

Jasmin smiled. It was a vibrant smile that lit up her entire face. "I do love my work very much. What do you do?"

"I run an advertising agency."

"Sounds like a busy job."

"It is."

"Get out much?"

"Not really."

"Well, the food bank's having a fund drive at the end of May. Want to come and support us?"

"Sure. That would be great. Thanks for inviting me."

"All right, sweetie. Time for a little touch football." From behind, Kristie grabbed Sara around the waist. "The key word being 'touch.' "

Sara tried to break free from her friend's grasp. "Kris!"

"C'mon, get up."

"I hate football," Sara protested.

"Yeah, but ya love me."

"You'd like to think so." Sara looked at Jasmin. She was laughing. "See what I have to put up with?"

Kristie stooped down and put her hand on top of Sara's shoulder. "A friend who loves you more than life itself."

Almost in shock, Sara looked up at Kristie, who suddenly let go of her. Emotion was so uncharacteristic for Kristie that Sara was at a complete loss for words.

Kristie turned away and picked up one of the footballs. "Well, are you guys gonna play or not?" She ran in the direction of the others and called out, "It's a goddamned beautiful day."

Sara sat immobilized and confused. At that moment, she felt many emotions. But for the first time in months, fear and loneliness were not among them.

The weekend and the picnic at the park faded into Sunday evening. Sara decided to do some work at the office when there would be no interruptions. It was quiet, eerily quiet, as she walked to her office.

During the day the workspace was one big buzz of voices, phones, faxes, copiers and movement up and down the aisles of cubicles. Being there alone was an entirely different experience. The isolation put her in a different mood. Over the large, quiet space, she felt little control. It was not a feeling she enjoyed. Sitting down at her desk, she turned on the computer. Selecting Microsoft Word from the toolbar, she brought up the list of documents in her electronic file folder. There were hundreds. Finally, after scrolling down the list, she found the one she was looking for: KodakStrategy. Opening the document, she quickly scanned the first ten pages. She had stopped working at the section which detailed the demographics breakout and consumer profile for individuals who had purchased a handheld camera in the past two years. Grabbing the manila file folder marked "demographics," she began perusing the various reports Paul had downloaded from their media consultant's most recent e-mail. Thumbing through the stapled pages, she realized there were several reports missing. She rummaged through the other stacks of papers on her desk, glanced over several other file folders and flipped through the mound of folders on the floor. The reports she needed were gone. Thinking that Paul might have borrowed them again, she got up and headed toward his office.

She flipped on his light switch and walked straight to his desk. It was annoyingly neat and orderly, not a paper out of place. Everything was stacked with precision, pages aligned perfectly, file tabs labeled in his clear, crisp handwriting. There was a photo in a walnut frame of his wife and two daughters. It was the perfect family to match the perfect desk. She looked around. It was an office that was almost clinical — without personality. Reference books were lined up by size, from largest to smallest. The coat rack was empty and a credenza was home to a computer that sat in pristine condition as though it had never been touched. Suddenly, she chuckled out loud. She wondered if the man ever did any real work.

Sara shuffled through the stack of files until she found what she was looking for. She pulled it from the pile, and another folder underneath fell to the floor.

"Damn," she said out loud. Getting down on her hands and knees, she began to reorganize the papers that had spread across the floor. A lone computer disk had also slid underneath Paul's chair. She grabbed it and threw it into the file folder. And then the label caught her eye. It read: "Memos to Richard Sanders." For a moment, she paused, very much confused. What memos to Richard Sanders? All of her account executives submitted their reports directly to her. Natalie compiled them every month and gave a summarized detail to the home office in San Francisco that included current projects, account activity, financial results and projections for the end of the quarter. Sara added any personnel issues, such as new hires and terminations. Those were the only reports she knew of that landed on Richard Sanders' desk.

Sara picked up the disk and read it again. "Memos to Richard Sanders." She got up and placed the file folder back on Paul's desk where she found it. Disk and demographic reports in hand, she went back to her office.

Sara inserted the floppy disk into the A drive. The drive clicked and whirred and the directory flashed on the screen. There was a list of at least forty documents called: GrayReport1, GrayReport2 and so on. The dates of the files went back almost a year.

Clicking on the first document, Sara waited nervously for it to open. It was dated September 26th. The memo header was addressed to Richard Sanders and the topic was "Executive President of Strategic Development." The body of the memo stated: "I wanted to inform you immediately of some disturbing incidences that have taken place in our office. Most of these difficulties, in my mind, can be traced to the office of Ms. Sara Gray, our executive president of strategic development. Ms. Gray, as you know, has been with the firm for approximately one year. During the course of this short tenure with our office, Ms. Gray has been consistently late arriving for work. When I have spoken to her on those mornings (see specific dates and times referenced below), she has been what I would describe as disoriented, confused and upset. One morning I noticed bruises on her face, which she had apparently tried to cover up and could not do so successfully. I bring these details to your attention only to keep you informed. In my opinion, no action is warranted at this time, but records of these types of incidences should be kept on file for obvious reasons."

Sara felt her stomach twirl into knots. She opened another memo dated only six months ago, just prior to her breakup with Joan.

"I am becoming more concerned about Ms. Gray's personal life — only in the context of its effect on her work and this office. Recently, she has called in sick with growing frequency (see specific dates and times referenced below) and is obviously under great personal duress. Due to some private investigation done on my own time, I can tell you that Ms. Gray is involved in an abusive relationship with another woman. While this is not reason for any kind of disciplinary action in and of itself because of the discriminatory repercussions which would follow, we need to take note of the effect this situation is having on our operations — and the effect it is having on Ms. Gray's ability to function on the job. At the very least, we should be counseling her and getting her the help she obviously needs. This may require her to relinquish (if only temporarily) some of her duties and assignments (such as the Kodak account), but, hopefully, only for a short period of time until her personal situation improves."

She couldn't read anymore. Not now. Quickly, Sara made a copy of the disk and put the original back in Paul's file folder. As stunned as she was, it wasn't hard for her to believe. What surprised her most was that she had never heard a word from Richard Sanders concerning these memos. Not a word. Was he planning on firing her after the Kodak account was won or lost? Sanders had known for many months the connections she had been able to establish at Kodak from the very first month she started her job. Was he waiting to give her the ax? Clearly, he knew she was a lesbian — and had been a battered one at that. Why no action? All of her conversations with him had been positive, upbeat. Was she being used until the pitch was complete? She wondered, now, if what might be her greatest achievement would also mark the end of her association with Partners Three. Kodak could be told that she had moved on of her own free will — and she would never say differently because of her own professional integrity. How many people knew? The entire staff? Her secretary? Yes, she had been ill. And yes there had been bruises. Some mornings she had been late because of fights with Joan, but many of those late mornings were also business-related meetings. Paul had colored it all to make it look like helpless irresponsibility. Anger coursed through her. She had survived it all only to discover that she hadn't survived anything. It felt like the final blow to her dignity.

Kristie sat in horrified disbelief as she listened to Sara's story about her discovery at the office. "Goddamned son-of-a-bitch. I always knew Paul was a snake. Let's go kill him now."

Sara curled up on Kristie's sofa. "Once this Kodak thing is all over with, I probably won't have a job. That's why Sanders showed up in Rochester — to find out where things stood. Once he realized that Kodak was giving us a shot because of the groundwork I had laid, he couldn't do anything. All he can do now is wait."

"That sucks. I'm so sorry, baby. After all you've been through—not this."

"Isn't it funny how Joan can still reach through the time and distance I've tried to put between us and still make my life a living hell?"

"I'm sorry. I really am."

"Well, I better get home."

"Too late for you to drive all the way across the city. You're not goin' anywhere."

"Okay. Just rustle me up a blanket and I'll pass out right here." Sara looked around the living room. There were newspapers, magazines and sale circulars stacked in various piles around the room. Dog toys littered the carpet. Ashtrays were overflowing. Old mail lay unopened on the two end tables. "I hardly think you'll even notice I'm here. About a week from now, you'll find me under a stack of old newspapers."

Kristie howled with laughter. "Good slam, my friend. Good slam. Okay, so I'm not the neatest person in the world. Some things just aren't a priority."

"It's okay. I love you anyway." Sara stepped on a gooey rawhide bone of Dudley's. "I think."

Sara lay on her side with Kristie's arm around her waist. She could hear Dudley snoring at the end of the bed. The room was completely dark and she was frightened. Kristie always turned a night-light on for her, but she had forgotten. The darkness tried to smother her, but she was too ashamed and embarrassed to say anything. Her heart pounded. She tried to concentrate on the sound of Dudley's snoring, but, suddenly, she gasped for breath.

Kristie jumped. "You all right?"

"I'm okay. Having trouble falling asleep." Sara started to shake uncontrollably.

"Hey, hey." Kristie pulled her close and kissed her forehead.

"I'm all right, really. The one thing I still have trouble with is sleeping."

"I know. You've slept here before." Kristie smacked her forehead. "Damn, baby. I forgot to turn on a light. Why didn't you say something?"

"Because it's ridiculous. I should be over this by now."

"The hell you should!" Kristie got up and switched on the night-light in the corner of the room near Sara. "I don't know what I was thinking. Mostly about how I'd like to kill that bitch. Damned fucking Joan. I hope an engine has run over her worthless ass by this time."

Sara chuckled.

"Well, I do, damnit."

"I know you do. And I appreciate that."

Kristie's eyes reflected the room's soft light. "You're so beautiful. I don't understand why someone who had the privilege of loving you chose to hurt you instead."

"Because she needed help."

"I'm glad you finally know that."

"Yes. I always thought it was me, but the counseling's taught me otherwise."

"The last thing on earth I want to see is you hurt again." Kristie kissed her nose and brushed the hair away from Sara's face. "I want you to find someone who will love you for the wonderful person you are."

"I'm sure that will happen someday."

"I know it will."

"Do you think we could have made it as a couple, Kris?"

Kristie leaned on one elbow. She thought for a few moments before answering. "I don't know, baby. Our lives are so intertwined. We rely on each other so much. Maybe we're too close." She looked down at Sara. "Does that sound stupid?"

"No." Sara put her hands over her face. "But I admit I sometimes get confused. I've learned to lean on you so hard."

"And that never needs to change. I'm always here for you, baby. Always."

Sara started to cry uncontrollably. She couldn't help herself. "I sometimes think I'm in love with you. You're so good to me and I need you so much."

"Shh. Okay. It's okay. Listen to me." Kristie put her hands on either side of Sara's face. "I love you. Do you understand that?"

"Yes. I really do."

"We've always loved each other. And you know what?"

"What?"

"We've learned from each other that love doesn't have to hurt. It doesn't have to come from anger. It can just come from itself and be what it should be. Beautiful like you." Kristie put her arms around Sara's waist. "It also doesn't have to be connected with making love or having sex."

Sara wiped her eyes with her T-shirt. "Well, I certainly know from firsthand experience that love and sex don't necessarily go together."

Kristie laid her head on the pillow. "You know, I've had such disastrous relationships. Women I really loved deeply. But something always seemed to go wrong. Somehow, it always ended up falling apart." Kristie's brown eyes turned almost black behind the shimmer of tears. "Then the person's lost to you forever. I don't want that to happen to us."

"I don't want that either."

"My love for you is deeper than what I've known in any relationship, Sara. Maybe I'm wrong. Maybe we could be lovers and live happily ever after. But for now, I'm not willing to take that risk. Are you?"

"No." Clutching Kristie's arms around her, Sara closed her eyes and fell asleep.

Two weeks later, Sara found herself on another plane. It was starting to be an unfortunate ritual.

Sara sat in the hospital room at her mother's bedside. Her mother was dying. Six months had suddenly become two weeks. Without warning, her second kidney failed and she had refused dialysis treatments. Hooked up to a dialysis machine was not how she wanted to live. Their last phone conversation from the previous weekend played over and over in Sara's mind. Her mother was in a state of confusion but still had moments of clarity, which Sara tried desperately to hang onto.

"Mom, how are you?"

"I'm okay. Really, Sara, it's not so bad."

"I wanted to call you and let you know I was thinking of you."

"Why don't you ever come into my room? Why do you call on the phone?"

"I'm in Atlanta, Mom. I couldn't get a seat on a plane for this weekend. I'm sorry."

"Well, I won't have my daughter standing on a plane."

"I'll be home next weekend."

"I don't want to be hooked up to machines, Sara. I'd rather face death now and have some dignity. I want it to be my choice — and the way I want to do it."

"I understand, Mom. It's just that I'm going to miss you so much."

"I know. But, it's not like I'm twenty-five years old, honey."

"Yes, I understand that."

"Will you do me a great honor?"

"Of course, Mom. Anything."

"You are so good at speaking. Such a poised young woman. You always have been and you've made me so proud. Will you speak at my memorial service? I've made some notes for you about some things I'd like you to say. Would that be all right?"

"Yes, Mom. I'll speak. Whatever you want. I love you," she said, hanging up the phone. Then she'd called Delta again to reconfirm her reservations.

Two of her brothers and her stepfather had just left. Her stepfather, crippled by Parkinson's Disease, could only visit the hospital for about twenty minutes at a time. But between all of them, they had kept a constant vigil at her mother's bedside.

She held her mother's hand and watched her sleep. She thought about what she would say at the service. Her mother was well-known in the community and had devoted most of her life to helping others. For almost 18 years, Elizabeth Gray had served as the executive director of a social service agency that offered programs to help the poorest of the poor: elderly, minorities, children. She was much beloved by many people and Sara wanted the tribute to be a fitting one. In her mind, as she sat there watching her mother die, she thought very much about how her mother had lived.

"Excuse me."

Startled, Sara looked up. A gray-haired, older gentleman dressed in a tweed suitcoat stood on the other side of her mother's bed. "Hi. Can I help you?"

The man extended his hand. "Yes, I'm Reverend Samuels. From the church. I stopped by to check on your mother."

"She sleeps a lot now."

"I know. I was here yesterday, too. The nurse said you'd gone to get something to eat." The reverend put his hand to her mother's forehead. "She seems comfortable."

"Yes, I think she is."

"How are you?"

"I'm okay, I guess. It's been hard on my whole family. We love her so much."

"Would you like to pray with me?"

"Yes, that would be comforting. Thank you."

The reverend leaned over the rail of the bed. "Elizabeth, it's Reverend Samuels. Your daughter is here and we're going to pray with you." The reverend took her mother's hand. "Dear Lord, please watch over our sister, Elizabeth. Her spirit is in your hands and we know that you will welcome her spirit into your loving house. Please also be with Elizabeth's family at this difficult time. May they be comforted in the knowledge that in your house there are many rooms, and that one is being prepared for Elizabeth. We ask for your comfort and peace in the name of your Son, Jesus Christ. Amen."

"Amen," Sara said haltingly. She could no longer control her emotions.

Suddenly, her mother's eyes opened. Her hands reached out and grabbed Sara's. "I'm going to miss you so much. I'm going to miss you so much."

Sara leaned over her mother's bed. "I'm going to miss you, too, Mom."

That was all her mother said. In a matter of moments, she had gone back to sleep.

The reverend shook her hand. "If you need anything at all, you call the church. You can leave a message if I'm not there."

"Thank you."

"I'll be back tomorrow."

"That would be fine. I'll be here."

Sara sat back down at her mother's bedside. She knew that her mother had heard the prayer and it seemed to comfort her. There was a smile on her face and a sense of peace had settled over the room. Sara took her mother's hand again. It was soft and warm. She held it up against her face and kissed each finger once. Resting her shoulder on the metal rail of the bed, she looked out the window behind her mother and watched the rain. Thousands of raindrops splashed onto the parking lot, matching the tears she cried now and knew she would cry in the days ahead.

Chapter Five

Buckhead, Atlanta's world-famous entertainment and shopping area, was jammed with people. The sunny, warm end-of-May weather and upcoming Memorial Day weekend had brought hordes of tourists to the city. Sara wandered into the restaurant and fought her way through another crowd until she spotted Jasmin across from the buffet tables. Jasmin was wearing a very tasteful black cocktail dress with a pearl necklace and earrings to match. She was involved in an animated discussion with several people until she looked up and saw Sara.

Smiling and nodding her head, she politely excused herself and quickly walked toward Sara. She smiled and Sara could suddenly feel the heat of this woman only a few inches away.

Her voice cracked when she spoke. "Hello. I made it."

"I'm so glad you did, Sara. I know how busy you are."

"Nice turnout."

"Yes, I'm really pleased. I think we're going to make our goal, for sure." Jasmin put her hand on Sara's shoulder. "There's a patio outside. Would you mind joining me? I need a break. I've been going nonstop for two hours here."

The patio was walled in by a brick façade covered with hanging plants in large, stucco pots. Climbing roses also were blooming along the patio wall. There were a few tables in the back corner away from the noisy crowd.

Jasmin sat down and sighed. Taking off a black leather pump, she stretched and wiggled her toes. "Ahhh. That feels good. God, I hate standing for hours in shoes like these."

Sara couldn't take her eyes off Jasmin. Her smile was infectious, her calm, quiet manner soothing and welcome in her turmoil-filled world. "It can be a killer."

"So, tell me how you've been since the picnic."

"Okay. Working hard. Long hours." Sara turned away and looked at the flowers again. They reminded her of her mother. Flowers had always been a gift her mother had enjoyed — for Easter, Mother's Day, her birthday. She especially enjoyed them the last few years when she could no longer do the flower gardening that had been a favorite hobby. But Sara didn't mention her mother to Jasmin. She wasn't sure she could without breaking down.

"Ever get any free time to just veg?"

"Rarely. My free time consists of going home after work and falling asleep in front of the TV or while hanging onto a good book."

Jasmin laughed, a dignified giggle that made Sara laugh. "I've been known to do that. Then I wake up and it's three a.m. and I wonder why I have a bedroom." Jasmin put her shoe back on and repeated the ritual with her other foot. She rubbed it and winced. "So, can I ask you a personal question, if you don't mind?"

"Sure."

"Are you and Kristie dating?"

Sara paused, not knowing what to say. Then she said what she felt was the honest truth. "Kristie and I have been friends for a long time — have been there for one another and are very close. We have a strong connection. It's a bond that I treasure."

"Well, is it okay if I ask you out? On a date, I mean. Would that be a problem?"

"Not in the context of Kristie and me."

"There wouldn't be another problem, would there?"

"Excuse me?"

"The fact that we're different races, maybe?"

"Oh, my. You mean because you're . . . no, not at all." Sara felt flustered. "Honest, I mean it didn't even occur . . . well, I mean, I noticed it, of course . . ." Sara put her hand to her forehead. "Good Lord, don't I sound stupid?"

Jasmin laughed and patted Sara's arm. "It's okay.

I know what you're trying to say. Just thought I'd ask. Some people might have a problem with it."

"Well, I'm not one of them."

"I know that." Jasmin rubbed the calf of her leg. "I find you very attractive, Sara. I thought we could just go out one night and have some fun. No pressure or anything. Just enjoy each other's company."

Sara struggled with a reply. "I'm flattered. Really I am."

"Why don't you think about it, okay? Here's my business card. Give me a call whenever you want — even if it's just to blab." Jasmin put the card in her hand. "It's okay. You really don't have to decide now."

Sara hated her hesitation. There was something special about this woman. "Thanks. I've just gotten over a difficult relationship. I haven't dated much — not real dates anyway."

"I understand. Hey, want to go back inside and get something to eat? The food's great — trust me on this." Jasmin got up and stretched across the table to the brick wall. She snapped a deep red rose off one of the vines. "Here, this will look great on your white jacket." She inserted the stem of the rose behind the gold pin on Sara's lapel.

"Thank you. That was very sweet."

"C'mon. You've got to taste this food."

"I am hungry."

"Well, dinner's on me, my friend."

* * * * *

The Tuesday after Memorial Day, Sara arrived at the office early. She sat stiffly, tapping her fingers on her desk. Sitting with his elbow resting on the arm of the office chair, Paul leaned his head into the palm of his hand. He looked indifferent, if not plain bored. Nothing she said seemed to make a difference. He was hell bent on this road to destroy her and was nearly succeeding — at least in destroying her confidence.

"Paul, I need to know if I'm going to have your support as we move forward with the Kodak project."

Paul rubbed his earlobe and shifted in his chair. "You know how I feel about how you've handled the Kodak account. I believe you should have allowed other members of the staff to take a greater role."

"I think *you* want a greater role and aren't so much concerned about the rest of the staff. And I've explained to you what I'd like your role to be."

"Perhaps you should tell me again so I'm more clear on what your expectations have been."

Sara drew little circles on a Post-It notepad. She needed this conversation first thing in the morning like she needed a hole in her head. "I discussed with you the importance of knowing you're here making sure our other clients are getting the same high-quality service they've come to expect." She glanced up at him. "I've also asked you to handle the overall operations on the management side — personnel matters, financial issues, that kind of thing. These are not small requests. It's a very important, crucial role. I don't understand why you feel so slighted."

Paul got up and started to pace in front of her

desk. The volume of his voice rose slightly. "I was here long before you arrived and I think I deserve to be involved in the more challenging aspects of client development." He stopped and extended his arm in her direction. "That's always been my goal and you know it. The Kodak account would have been a great way for me to show that my years of experience count in bringing in top clients."

"And you think handling the overall operational aspects of the business doesn't suit your skills? I think it taps into your greatest strengths."

With a look of disgust, Paul waved his hand at her. "Your opinion, I guess."

"Well, that's the recommendation I've made to the home office, and so far I haven't heard anything to make me believe they'd like to see things run differently." Sara folded her hands on top of her desk. "I've been given pretty much free rein to run the business as I see fit."

Clearly angry, Paul snapped one of his suspenders against his chest. "So, what are you telling me?"

"That until I hear otherwise, I want your cooperation."

Snap went the suspender again. "Well, until you hear otherwise, I guess I don't have much choice."

"No, you don't."

Her mother died on the following Wednesday at 5:25 in the evening. Sara was in Atlanta, 800 miles away. At seven o'clock, her brother called to tell her. He was still at the hospital.

"Are you okay?" he asked.

"I guess so."

"Listen, Sara. This may sound like a stupid idea, but I'm worried that you're so far away. Here's what I'd like to do and you tell me if you want to, okay?"

"Okay."

"I'm going to go back to Mom's room and call you from the phone next to her bed. Then, I'll hold the phone up to Mom's ear so you can say good-bye. Would you like to do that?"

Sara closed her eyes and clenched her jaw. "Yes."

"I'll call you right back."

In a few minutes, the phone rang again.

"I'm in Mom's room now, Sara. I'm going to put the phone next to her ear, and you say what you want to say."

"Okay." There was a rustling sound at the other end of the line. Sara waited a few seconds. She imagined her mother's spirit hovering somewhere in the room, waiting for her to say good-bye. "Mom, it's Sara. I want you to know that you were the love of my life and I'm going to miss every day without you. I'm going to miss your strength and your laughter and our quiet times together. The lunches we enjoyed on Saturdays . . . the shopping trips to the mall . . . the long rides in the country . . . the days in the mountains. Remember, you're safe in my heart. Always. Rest now, Mom. Good-bye."

The weekend prior to her mother's death, Sara had stayed overnight in the hospital room. For two days, she and her brothers had kept an uneasy vigil. Her mother slept most of the time and said little. Once, she woke up suddenly and called out, "Sara!"

Sara jumped from the small, uncomfortable cot near her mother's bedside. "It's okay, Mom, I'm here."

"Sara, I'm losing my heart! I'm losing my heart!"

Taking her mother's hand, Sara said, "No, Mom. You've still got your heart. It's right here." Sara rested her mother's hand on her chest. "And I've got your heart, too." She put her mother's hand over her own heart. "It's here — safe inside me forever."

"I can't find the lake."

For many years, her mother and stepfather owned a cabin located on the shores of Lake Wallenpaupack in the beautiful Pocono Mountains of Pennsylvania. Sara sat down next to her mother's bed. "Oh, the lake's right outside the window of our cabin, Mom. See how blue the water is? We're sitting on the back steps, talking about the kids and how much fun we had that day. About going inside and building a fire just before dinner. It's late spring there now. The evening air's cool and the leaves of the trees are rustling in the night air. The mountain laurel and the rhododendron are blooming. And before you know it, the kids will be swimming in the lake and we'll sit on the shore and listen to them laugh and splash. And we'll laugh, too."

As though she were drifting back to that peaceful time when the moments seemed to stop, frozen by the tranquil beauty of that place, her mother smiled. Sara thought about what she had just said. Yes, the mountains had come back to life . . . just as her mother's life was fading away. It was all happening too quickly and she wanted it to stop. Why couldn't she make it all stop? The spiraling seconds that were taking her mother's life were obliterating what little was left of her own spirit. While her mother's spirit lifted itself to another place, she knew that hers would stay and linger, so much heavier than it had ever been before.

More than three hundred people gathered for the memorial service planned in her mother's honor. She and her brothers had picked some of her mother's favorite hymns — "How Great Thou Art," "Amazing Grace," "The Old Rugged Cross." The flowers were bright and colorful — all the varieties her mother loved — carnations, spider mums, gladiolas. The only flowers missing were lilies. Her mother had hated lilies.

Sara walked to the podium and looked out over the crowd of people which included relatives, friends, co-workers, civic leaders and community police. Many of her mother's clients, the impoverished people of the government housing project where her mother had worked, were also there. These hundreds of people, she thought, represented the richness of her mother's life of service to others. A surge of pride coursed through her as she spoke of the woman they had joined together to honor.

In a strong, clear voice she said, "Elizabeth Gray was an extraordinary woman. Never was this more evident than in her last days when she looked death in the eye and refused to blink. It was clear that she was going to die as she had lived — on her own terms. As selfless as my mother was, the last and final thing she did, she did for herself. She refused the painful treatments she did not want — and made herself ready."

As she spoke, flashes of her mother came and went. A beautiful teenager, wearing a black dress and pearls, standing on the sidewalk in front of her grandparents' house. A young woman holding her baby brother, smiling for the camera her father held. A civic leader standing at a podium, speaking with pride at her social service agency's tenth anniversary dinner.

"In her last days, my mother asked me to tell her clients of the Marvine-Pembroke neighborhood how much she loved you. She loved all of you. She wanted me to tell you that it was you who gave her faith and hope. That through you, she gained the strength to keep going — even in the last two years when she was often tired and not feeling well. My mother did not want to quit, because you never quit. I ask you now, in her memory, not to quit. Keep on going and help and love one another."

She remembered a woman who, with great strength and courage, faced the loss of one husband and the debilitating disease of another. A woman who fought hunger and AIDS and poverty and discrimination and government bureaucracy for those who could not fight.

"My mother was no candle in the wind. My mother was the wind. I will remember her mostly for her strength. In her voice, you could hear that strong will, that indomitable spirit. But she always managed to blend that strength with compassion, a sharp wit, humor and a genuine caring for others. It was a beautiful blending of a spirit that touched us all."

Sara was overcome with an incredible emptiness at the very core of her soul. She struggled to feel her mother's presence somewhere in that sanctuary — in the eyes of the people who loved her, in the scent of the flowers she once grew in her own garden, in the sound of the music she had sung to her as a child. But she could not find her and she felt a terrible panic. Mechanically, and with little comfort, she stumbled through her final words.

"We will all miss the strong wind that was my mother. We will miss her strength that had become a refuge and a comfort for so many. But the love she gave to us will lift us up, and the strength she passed onto us will keep us steady. Now is the time for us to give thanks and celebrate her wonderful, precious life. That was her final wish. 'Have a party and celebrate my life,' she said. 'I have no regrets. I have done all that I wanted to do and more.' "

Regrets? Sara had a thousand. And then a million. And they were all packaged in moments — the moments she faced ahead without the loving presence of her mother. How could she move forward and endure the days to come?

"Mom, today we celebrate your life. Through your love and untamed will, we have all been truly blessed."

There was a quiet hush as she gathered her papers together and stepped down from the podium. *Good-bye, Mom,* she thought. *Your heart is safe. It beats with mine.*

Chapter Six

The club was crowded for a Thursday night with people starting their weekend early. Sara stood at the bar, watching Kristie dance with several women who were weekend regulars. The music was a mix of Prince songs, only a few of which Sara recognized. She felt disconnected from the music, the people, herself.

"Hey, baby. Going to dance with me?" Kristie asked.

"Not really in the mood. I don't know why I'm

here. I guess I didn't feel like just sitting at home doing nothing. That seemed like a worse alternative."

Kristie gave her a hug. "There's nothing I can say to take away your pain, except that I'm here for you. I know you were very close to your mom. I'm sure you're going to miss her a lot."

"I already do."

"I'm sorry this happened. Especially now, when you're still struggling to rebuild your life."

"I'll be okay."

"Come to my office with me. I want to talk to you."

"Okay."

The office was a mess. There was no better word to describe it. Empty boxes were piled on the floor. Filing cabinets were open with folders stacked on top of the ones that were filed. Dirty ashtrays, filled to the brim, were on every conceivable surface. Bills and shipping receipts littered the desk. Sara thought it was a desk. She couldn't see past the clutter to know.

"Kris, how do you function?"

"Excuse me?" Kristie moved a half-full Styrofoam coffee cup. It was filled with old cigarette butts.

"How do you work in here?"

Kristie lit a cigarette. "Aw, hell. It ain't hard. You just shove things around until you find what you're looking for."

Sara sat in the office chair next to the desk. It wobbled so much, it almost threw her to the floor. "God!"

"Kinda like breakin' in a new horse, huh?"

Sara shook her head and laughed. "The trials of

business ownership. Some things just aren't important."

"That's right." Kristie reached out and brushed Sara's cheek lightly with her hand. "But you are. I hope you know that."

"I'm what?"

"Very important to me."

"Yes, I know that."

"About what happened that night a few weeks ago . . ."

Sara held up her hands, pressing against the air with her fingertips. "Kris, it's okay."

"Well, we haven't had a chance to talk since your mom died. After we spoke so openly about our feelings for each other, I thought I might have hurt you. That you might have taken it as a rejection." Kristie leaned her head into her hands. Her face looked worn. "I love you to death, Sara. I want to make sure you understand that."

"I know you do, Kris. What I think is that we're two very good friends who are a little confused right now." Sara got up and, stepping over some mounds of paper, looked at the photographs on the wall to the right of the desk.

"Yes, I guess we are."

"I love you too, Kris. But quite frankly, I don't know how I feel or what I want. Way too much has happened. So, please don't worry about it."

"Okay. Whatever you say."

"Thanks for your concern."

Sara straightened one of the dozens of photographs dating back ten years to the original opening of the bar. In one photo, Kris stood outside in front of the building, looking proud and confident.

And so young. Sara felt Kristie's arms wrap around her shoulders.

"I love you."

"I love you, too." Sara turned and faced her friend. Suddenly, she wanted nothing more than to get out of that office. Confusion reigned. "You better get some work done — if you can find it."

Kristie kissed her forehead. "Very funny."

"I'm going to go grab a beer."

"Okay. Be out later. Need to make some quick phone calls."

Sara leaned up against the bar, gulping down a beer. In between gulps, she peeled the label from the bottle, one corner at a time. She thought about her mother and how much she missed her. She thought about the feelings she had for Kristie, how confused her love for her had become, like so many other things in her life. An emptiness inside her left an ache so painful it made her physically sick. The two most important people in her life — her mother and Kristie — seemed lost to her. The loss of her mother was hard enough, but the loss of her friendship with Kristie would be more than she could ever bear. She and Kristie had approached that fine line that sometimes occurred between friends, and she wondered what would happen if they ever stepped across it. Would they be able to step back into just being friends again? Without hurt? Without resentment? Did she even want to step over the line? Was her love for Kristie something more? Or was her life in such disarray that Kristie seemed like the comfortable answer? Her head was spinning. Maybe it was the beer. She tried to focus her vision on the wall across the room. What she saw was a bad dream. She put her beer bottle down, convinced there was something in it, some mind-altering drug that was making her see things. And then the vision moved and she knew in that instant that the nightmare she had feared for so long was walking toward her with an all-too-familiar directness.

"Sara, it's been a while. How are ya?" Joan loomed in front of her, dressed in black denim jeans and a blue denim shirt, embroidered with an Atlanta Braves logo. Sara felt like the Braves tomahawk symbol was poised at her throat.

Sara took a step backward. "Joan, you need to go. We have nothing to say to each other."

Joan swiped at the air with her hand. "Aw, c'mon. All that stuff's in the past. I just wanna know how you're doin."

Sara measured her words carefully. "I'm doing okay."

Joan smiled and nodded. "Good. I mean that. I'm glad if you're happy."

"Well, I'm not exactly happy, Joan. My mother just died."

Joan appeared genuinely shocked. "Oh, Jesus. When did that happen?"

"Not long ago."

"Sara, I'm awfully sorry." Joan slapped the surface of the bar with her hand. "Honest, I am. I know how close you and your mom were."

"Thanks."

"How's Kristie?"

"Why do you ask? In fact, I'm surprised to see you here at her place."

"I'm waitin' for a friend."

"Good for you."

Joan shoved her hands into her pockets. "Well, that's not exactly true. I was kinda hopin' to see you here."

"Why?"

"To apologize. For all the trouble. I know that sounds lame now. But I really mean it."

"It comes far too late, Joan."

"Now, why do you have to be like that? I'm tryin' to be nice here." A flash of the old Joan.

"It doesn't matter. None of it matters anymore."

"Matters to me."

"Well, it doesn't to me. Anyway, I was just about to leave. Take care of yourself."

Joan's hands were suddenly in the air. "Hey, wait a minute. You don't have to go just 'cause of me. Talk with me for a few minutes. How's your job?"

Sara stepped to one side. "It's okay. I've really got to go."

Joan stepped in front of her and grabbed her arm. "I said, don't go. I wanna talk to you."

"Let go of my arm, Joan. Those days are gone forever. I don't have to put up with this anymore."

Joan squeezed harder. "That's just like you, Sara. Damn—you always aggravated the situation. Made every goddamned thing worse. Maybe it wouldn't have been so bad if you'd been more fuckin' understandin'."

"If you're saying that I provoked you into physically abusing me, Joan, that's a pile of crap." Sara could feel her eyes burning with anger. Her eyelid was twitching out of control. "You're an abuser, Joan. You can't control your behavior and you need to get help. I'm sick of taking the blame. Get the fuck out of my way now! I mean it. Let go of my arm and get out of my way."

As if staggered by a blow, Joan let go and backed up.

Sara moved cautiously, walking around Joan and bumping right into Kristie.

Kristie put her hands on Sara's waist to steady her. "You all right?"

"I'm fine."

"Joan, what are you doing here? How 'bout finding the front door?"

"Fuck you. I'll leave when I'm goddamned good and ready."

Sara turned and looked Joan straight in the eye. "Leave, Joan. Don't even think about starting anything. I just told you, I don't have to take your shit anymore. Don't ever come near me again."

Joan stared at Kristie, her dark eyes turning cold. Then she shrugged and said, "No problem. This place is a goddamned dump anyway."

Kristie and Sara stood side-by-side, watching Joan walk toward the exit.

"Are you leaving?" Kristie asked.

Sara nodded. "Yes. Suddenly, I'm very tired."

"C'mon, then. I'll walk you to your car."

"No, it's okay. I'll be fine."

Kristie put her arm around Sara's shoulder. "I'll walk you to your car. Humor me, okay?"

"Okay." Sara put two dollars on the bar and followed Kristie out the door.

The parking lot was wet from an earlier rain.

Kristie took Sara's hand as they slogged through the puddles together.

"Stay at my house tonight."

"Why?"

"Because I know how upset you are."

"I'm okay."

"Then why is your hand shaking?"

"I'm cold."

"It's eighty degrees out, Sara." Kristie opened the car door for her. "You have a key. Let yourself in, okay? Be home in an hour or so. You'll do this for me, won't you? You know how much I'll worry."

"See you later."

An hour later, Sara lay in Kristie's room fighting off thoughts of Joan and the three years of hell they had spent together. Was there ever a peaceful time, she thought, when things had been good between them? Maybe at the beginning, that first year when Joan seemed like a different person, calm, attentive and loving. But there had always been a seething just beneath the surface of Joan. A personality that seemed ready to explode under any kind of pressure.

The shirt Joan was wearing at the bar that night made her think about the baseball game. It was a perfect example of Joan's fragile temperament. Joan had gotten them wonderful seats from the fire station chief. They sat at the club level of Turner Field in the brand new stadium, home to the Atlanta Braves. The place was packed for an early season game against the St. Louis Cardinals. The crowd had just finished doing the wave as the game moved into the third inning. The Braves were batting and Joan was yelling, excited and really into the action. As usual, Sara was thinking about her job and not really paying attention to what was going on. The Braves must have gotten a hit because Joan turned to her and said, "Did you see that? Isn't this great?"

"What?"

"The game. Isn't this fun?"

Sara tried to snap herself out of a work-induced stupor. "Oh, yes. Beautiful field."

Joan was immediately angry. "Are you watchin' the goddamned game or what?"

"Of course I am."

"The hell you are. You're thinkin' about that fuckin' job of yours."

"Well, I was just for a second. But I really am enjoying the game."

"Goddamnit, Sara. I work my fuckin' ass off to get these tickets for us — and you're not even payin' attention."

Sara felt the beads of sweat pop along her forehead. "I am paying attention. Now we're both missing the game."

Joan pounded her fist on her knee. "Why do you do this to me?"

"What are you talking about?"

"Put me down."

"I haven't put you down."

"Not in words, but in goddamned actions. What, you too good to go to a fuckin' baseball game with me? It's not the femme thing to do, or what?"

Sara put her head in her hands. There were people all around them and she was sure they were listening. "Don't be ridiculous."

"I know, I know," Joan said in a sarcastic tone.

"At your job they give you tickets to the Fox and overnight stays at the Westin. Well, I'm sorry if goin' to a baseball game is beneath you, Miss Victoria."

"Joan, knock it off. Watch the game. I do appreciate the tickets and I was having fun until you started this argument."

Joan shot up from her seat. "Don't tell me what I goddamned started! Fuckin' bitch. We're leavin'."

Sara looked around her. People were staring at them, obviously annoyed. "Joan, please. You're making a scene. C'mon. Sit down. I want to watch the game."

"I said we're leavin'." Joan grabbed Sara by the arm and yanked her from her seat.

"Joan, let go. You're hurting my arm."

The gentleman sitting next to Sara stood up. "Hey, let go of her." He pointed his finger at Joan. "I've had just about enough of you. Can't you see we're all trying to watch the game here? Sit down and shut up already."

"Don't tell me what to do, ya big creep. Mind your own goddamned business."

"Lady, if you don't let go of her, I'm going to call security."

Joan pushed Sara away. "Fine, bitch. See how ya like walkin' home."

Joan stomped off and Sara sat back down in her seat, totally humiliated. She fought back tears.

"Hey, lady. You okay? Need help?" the man next to her asked.

"No, thank you. I'll be all right."

Sara got up, negotiating her way across the long row of people. She left the stadium and walked to the MARTA station. She had taken the train to the stop located about a mile from Kristie's house. It was a ten-minute ride to the same place she always ran, the very same place she found herself now.

She drifted off to sleep. Sometime later, she felt the presence of Kristie as she slipped into bed next to her.

"You okay?"

"Now that you're here I am."

"Sorry you had to go through that tonight," Kristie said softly. "Must've been really hard."

"It was painful, yes. All the familiar fears came rushing back, and I felt like that same old person again."

"But you weren't that same person, Sara. You stood up for yourself."

"Did I?"

"You did. I was so damned proud of you."

"I was too frightened to even know what I was saying. Really, I just wanted to get away from her."

"You did great."

"Thanks. Maybe I've actually learned something in the past six months."

"You have. You've learned how to live again."

Sara put her arms around Kristie's neck. "Why do I feel I need to let go of you? But I just can't right now."

"You don't have to let go. I'm here for you."

Trying to recover from her mother's death was like trying to learn how to walk again, think again, feel again. Much to her surprise, the process of healing was directly connected to the comforting presence of Jasmin Matthews. Since the week before Memorial Day, in between her trips to Pennsylvania, she and Jasmin had seen each other several times — for lunch, dinner, drinks.

From the 74th floor of Atlanta's Westin Hotel, the entire city was visible. The circular building's scenic elevator had brought them to the highest floor to the bar that slowly rotated, with a clear night view of the city's most beautiful buildings and popular sights. Sara, already mesmerized by the Atlanta skyline, was finding it difficult to focus, but even the beauty of the city at night could not compete with the attractiveness of the woman sitting across from her.

"I thought you'd enjoy the view. This is one of my favorite places," Jasmin said, sipping a margarita.

"And I thought the city was beautiful from ground level—but this is really breathtaking. Do you have any other secret spots?"

"I do. And I plan to take you to every one of them." Jasmin shifted uncomfortably in her chair. "Sara, why didn't you ever tell me about your mother?"

Sara looked up into those earth-brown eyes. She almost forgot the question. "How did you know?"

"I called your office to ask you to lunch. They said you were out of town at your mother's funeral." Jasmin set her glass on the table. "I want you to know how sorry I am."

Sara started to peel the label from her beer bottle. "Thank you. I should have said something. Just couldn't."

"You've got to be ready to talk about something like that."

"My mother and I were extremely close. When

she died, I wanted to run away from everything and everyone. But I couldn't, and I knew it." Sara fought back tears. "With all that's been happening in my life right now, I haven't even had time to mourn."

"You've got to take the time to do that, Sara. It's important."

"I know."

"Do you have a big family?"

Sara crumpled up the peeled beer label and tossed it into the ashtray. "Three brothers. Three sisters-in-law I love to death. And six nephews and a niece. Also my stepfather."

"Do they all live in Pennsylvania?"

"Yes. About an hour and a half northwest of Philadelphia."

"And do you always peel the labels off beer bottles?"

Sara smiled sheepishly. "Only when I'm nervous."

"Why are you nervous?"

"Because I'm really attracted to you and, quite honestly, I don't want to be."

"Why not?"

Sara sighed and sat back in her chair. For a moment, her gaze strayed toward the thousands of lights that stretched south toward Hartsfield International Airport. "A little over six months ago I finally got out of a very abusive relationship. I go to group therapy once a week."

Jasmin appeared shocked. "That's awful. My God, you've been through so much." She reached for Sara's hand and held it firmly. "I'm so glad you're moving past that terrible situation."

"It surprises you, doesn't it?" Sara heard the edge in her own voice. Felt the anger flashing in her eyes. She wondered if Jasmin would notice it.

Jasmin shook her head. "Sadly, it happens to people like you everyday. My work with the Food Bank exposes me to many worlds, good and bad. Some worlds I've never known—only heard about." Jasmin let go of Sara's hand and picked up her drink. "People have this perception that if you're black, you must have grown up poor. I came from a middle-class family where times were sometimes rough, yes. But we were also sheltered from a lot. We had food, clothes, went to school, college. My parents were solid people. They worked hard." Crossing her legs, Jasmin said, "My point is that perceptions are just that — perceptions. You don't have to be black to be poor. You don't have to be married to a truck driver and have three kids to be beaten."

"I'm sorry. Every once in a while I slip into that anger mode."

"That's understandable. You must feel a lot of anger."

"I only wanted you to know why I'm hesitant to get back into the dating scene, as it were. But maybe it's time. There's so much upheaval in my life right now, change and looking ahead are good things, I think."

"But sometimes scary."

"Yes."

"Do you want to get together again?"

"I'd like that very much."

* * * * *

Karen fidgeted in the seat next to her, chain-smoking as usual, her brown eyes shifting nervously around the room. The Tuesday night meeting hadn't started yet. Sara had come straight from work and was still dressed in her gray pants suit.

"You look so pretty all dressed up like that."

Sara was startled by the shy woman's declaration. "Why, thank you, Karen. But I feel a little out of place. I didn't have time to stop home and change."

"I don't have to dress up for my job. Just slip my greens on over jeans and a top."

"That's right. You work in a hospital."

"Yep. In the neo-natal care unit. I help take care of the little ones."

"You like it?"

For the first time, Sara saw Karen smile. "Oh, yeah. I love the babies." Karen took a long drag on her cigarette. "I had a baby of my own once, but she got taken."

"Taken?"

"Uh huh. My ex-husband took her when she was three. Got custody 'cause I moved in with my girlfriend."

"Do you still see her?"

"Not much. He moved to California. I used to see her 'round the holidays. Talked to her on the phone a little." Karen's hands started to shake. "Then my girlfriend started beating me up. She didn't want me talking to my ex-husband or my daughter. So I've kind of lost touch now."

"I'm sorry."

"He moved again. My ex-husband, that is. Don't even know the phone number." Karen ground out the cigarette stub. "But maybe it's better that way. And I still have my babies at work."

"Yes, you do."

The rest of the group started to take their seats and Dr. Langford joined the circle.

"Evening, ladies. Who would like to start?"

"I think Sara should start," Vanessa said, her hands resting on top of her head. "She's got a story to tell."

Sara had bumped into Vanessa in the lobby before the meeting. She mentioned her run-in with Joan.

"Have something to share, Sara?" the doctor asked politely.

"Yes, actually I do."

"This is good," Vanessa said, lifting her long hair up off her neck. She let it go and it bounced softly around her face again. "Run-in with the ex."

There were some audible gasps.

"You saw Joan?" Karen asked.

"Yes, I ran into her at Kris's club this past week."

Vanessa leaned forward. She was chewing gum a mile a minute. "Tell all, girl."

"I was standing at the bar at Kris's and suddenly she was there, leaning up against the wall across the room. It took a few seconds for my eyes to tell my brain it was actually her." Sara took a deep breath, remembering the moment. "She approached me and I almost panicked. But I knew if I did, I'd be giving over that control again — the control she wanted. I asked her why she was there, and she told me she was waiting for a friend."

"Yeah, right," Karen said, lighting another

cigarette. "From what you've always said, she hates Kristie. She'd never go there except to look for you."

Sara laughed. "You're right. She admitted that she was looking for me, that the waiting-for-a-friend line had been a lie."

"So, what'd you say to her?" Kim asked.

"I told her that we had nothing to say to each another. Eventually, the charming Joan went away, and the old Joan showed herself."

Dr. Langford took off her jacket and hung it on the back of her chair. "Which Joan was that, Sara?"

"The Joan that was always angry. She grabbed my arm when I said I was leaving. She tried to blame all of our problems on me. I told her she was the one with the problem. I called her an abuser. I told her she needed help."

"Wow!" Vanessa popped her gum and rested her chin in her hand. "What did she say?"

Sara shrugged. "Nothing. And then she did something she's never done before. She stepped backward, away from me. She let go of my arm. I walked around her and she didn't move."

"Why do you think she backed away?" the doctor asked.

"I think she finally knew that she didn't have that power over me anymore. The sound of my voice — the fact that I told her exactly what I thought she was. Actually, it was kind of sad."

"Shit, girl. You got to be kidding!" Vanessa threw her hands up in the air. "You felt sorry for her?"

"Yes. I felt sorry for her." Folding her arms across her chest, Sara shook her head. "Don't misunderstand me. Nothing can ever excuse what she did to me. Nothing. But I suddenly have a very clear perspective of the hell I lived through with Joan and the cycle I was a part of." Sara looked around the room. "The cycle we've all been a part of." She bit down on her bottom lip. "Just like all of you, I'm the victim of a victim of a victim of a *victim.*" Sara put her head in her hands. She couldn't stop thinking the word. "Victims of all the women like Joan and where they came from. From families that perpetuated violence all through childhood." She looked up and said, "Like an alcoholic father who beat his twelve-year-old daughter with a belt and threw her out of the house so many times, Joan lost count. The same young girl who ended up in the hospital twice when her father wrecked the car because he'd been drinking. A young girl beaten so bad that she couldn't sit down in school — so she stood in the back of the room for two days. She told the teacher she'd fallen, and that's how she hurt herself." Sara leaned back in her chair and closed her eyes. "In my mind, for so long there was no connection. It was just me — and what I was doing wrong to provoke this horrible behavior." Tears ran down her face. Karen reached over and dabbed her cheeks with a tissue. "Joan's mistake was not getting the help she needed to heal, to recover that self-esteem she'd lost so long ago. Instead, she tried to take mine, and that was wrong. And until she gets the help she needs, she'll continue to beat the self-esteem out of every woman she attempts a relationship with. And that will be wrong, too. There's no excuse for not getting help. No excuse for using excuses to beat the hell out of someone. That's where the cycle has to end. With the abuser. And with the victim."

"The victim?" Kim asked.

Sara ran her hands through her hair. "Well, don't we have a responsibility, too?" Sara slapped her hands on her thighs. "Isn't it up to us to recognize that it's not us? That we are not responsible — and get the hell on with our lives?"

The room was suddenly quiet.

"Thank you, Sara," Dr. Langford finally said. "Anyone else?"

Chapter Seven

Richard Sanders was cleaning his glasses with a handkerchief when Sara walked into her office on Wednesday morning. She shut the door and sat down at her desk. Another surprise visit. Another unscheduled meeting.

"How are you, Richard?"

Sanders squinted through each eyeglass lens, holding his glasses at a distance, before putting them back on. "Just fine, Sara. I'm just fine." He smiled and looked up, then folded his hands on top of his knee. "Here I am again without warning," he said matter-of-factly. "I really don't enjoy doing this, you know."

"What can I help you with, Richard?"

"First of all, I wanted to express my sincerest sympathies on the recent death of your mother. I'm so very sorry."

Sara swallowed hard. "Thank you, Richard. I appreciate it."

"I also wanted to check on how things were going with Kodak. Paul pretty much filled me in before you got here."

Sara flinched. "Did he?"

"Yes. He says you've picked your team for the presentation next month."

"I have."

Sanders cleared his throat. "Paul seems quite unhappy with your choices."

"I'm sorry he feels that way. I, on the other hand, feel extremely confident and proud of the caliber of people we can assemble for this opportunity." Sara pointed to the creative boards, layouts, detailed comps and proposals that were strewn across her desk. "And the work that's been done is some of the finest I've ever seen."

"I'm glad you feel so confident." Sanders leaned forward and grabbed one of the print ads. While he reviewed the work, he said, "Do you think, however, that it's wise to represent the agency with only one senior member of this staff? That senior member being you, of course."

"Not at all. I know the people at Kodak. They'll expect me to be carrying the ball."

"And you feel comfortable doing that?"

"Of course. Why do you ask?"

Sanders slid the display board back onto Sara's desk. "Well, some of us are meant to pave the way — to generate the opportunity. And some of us are better suited to present the blood-and-guts information."

"What are you saying, Richard?"

"Nothing. I just wanted your take on the team you've assembled for this important task."

"The best in the business. That's my take. I stand behind my choices — and behind everyone on the team."

Sanders nodded affirmatively. "Very well, then. I do have a suggestion, however."

"I'm open to any suggestions you have, Richard."

"I'd like Paul to be involved in the process from here on in as far as the formal presentation to Kodak goes." Sanders appeared uncomfortable, almost squirming in his chair. "You need to have a backup in case something comes up. God forbid, but you could become ill, or have another family emergency. We need someone ready to step in and take over for anyone on the team. I think Paul's well suited to handle any aspect of the presentation."

"Yes, of course. I'll make sure Paul's involved in all the critical meetings leading up to the presentation."

"Good."

"Thank you for flying in to give your support. It's greatly appreciated."

"Certainly." Sanders uncrossed his legs and leaned forward. "I also want to say that I know about the problems in this office, particularly between you and Paul. I don't want to get into details about any of this, except to say that I don't expect any difference of business philosophies to in any way interfere with our opportunity to win the Kodak account. Am I being clear?"

"Yes, Richard. I've worked very hard to make certain that doesn't happen. There are problems, yes, but none that can't be resolved and certainly none that will affect this upcoming opportunity."

"Good. You'll keep me informed of our progress?"

"Of course. Are you planning on attending the formal pitch to Kodak?"

"Yes, I'll be there. Wouldn't miss it. It's going to be very exciting, I think. Don't you?"

"Absolutely. We'll be ready."

"I'm counting on it." With that, he stood up and left her office.

Kristie was hunched over her desk, cigarette dangling from her mouth as she punched away at an adding machine. Rolls of paper from the machine had cascaded onto the floor.

"Hi, Kris. Is this a bad time?"

Kristie looked up and smiled. As she talked, cigarette ashes scattered across the desk. "Not at all, baby. Just addin' up the profits." Kristie roared with laughter.

Sara was confused. "Did I miss something?"

"That was a joke, honey. These are the bills!" Kristie reeled in the roll of adding machine paper. "Man, I better start waterin' down the drinks." She looked up and laughed again. "But then I'd have to fire Rick. He prides himself on his drink-making abilities. Ever taste one of his own concoctions?"

Sara giggled. "No, I stick with beer."

"Good. A wise move." Kristie put her feet up on the desk. "How's it goin' at work? Do I need to buy stock in Kodak yet?"

"Not yet. I'll sure be glad when it's over."

"No doubt. Hey, you doin' anything tomorrow night?"

"Nope."

"Good. Come by the house and I'll make dinner for you."

Sara's mouth dropped. Kristie was the worst cook she'd ever known. "Dinner?"

"Don't worry, doll. I'm just gonna reheat some leftover pizza."

They both laughed. "In that case, I'll be there." Sara stepped over a pile of promotional flyers and left.

Later that evening, Sara fell asleep on the sofa watching TV. The phone rang and she woke up suddenly, thinking it was her alarm clock. When she realized she was in the living room, she groped for the portable phone.

"Sara, it's Jennifer. Did you hear?"

"Jennifer? Hi." Sara rubbed her eyes. "What's up?"

"Did I wake you? Oh, God, you haven't heard then."

"Heard what?"

"Listen, I don't know how to tell you this, but you need to get to the nightclub right away."

Sara froze. "Why? What's happened?"

"It's been bombed."

Sara held the phone away from her ear and looked at it. Surely she was dreaming. "Jennifer, where are you?"

"Home. Had the night off. Rick just called. He says everything's bedlam there. Cops all over the place. People hurt."

"Kris?"

"I don't know."

"I'm on my way."

Bomb? People hurt? Kristie? It was a frantic ride all the way to the bar. Sara paid no attention to the speedometer. She kept her eyes glued to the road, while her heart stayed lodged in her throat. She just couldn't believe it. My God, she had just been there earlier that evening. Joking with Kristie, laughing and being silly. Tears pooled in her eyes.

As she turned onto the street where the club was located, Sara felt another surge of panic. Already she could see the flashing lights — as far as several blocks away from the building. Realizing she couldn't get the car any closer, Sara pulled over to the curb.

She broke into a run, trying to get as close as she could on foot. When she finally reached the actual block the club was on, she could see that people were everywhere, mingling in groups. People who worked at the nearby restaurants and convenience stores, along with their patrons, had flooded the streets. Police cars were parked diagonally across the road and officers were frantically trying to clear people and cars from the scene. Ambulances were lined up beyond yards and yards of yellow tape. Paramedics waited in the street — some pacing back and forth, others emptying the trucks of equipment. About a block away, she ran into police barricades.

"Sorry, miss. You can't go any farther," an officer said.

"My best friend owns this place."

"Sorry. Nothing I can do. You really need to move back."

Sara watched in horror as the police combed the outside of the building with flashlights, digging through shrubbery, garbage, looking under parked vehicles. Did they think there were more bombs? Fire trucks were situated in the lot on the west side of the structure. There was an acrid smell of smoke. Sara jumped on top of the hood of a nearby car to get a better look. That's when she saw the real damage to the double-story building. What used to be The Patio was now a tangled mass of wood and metal. And that's when the awful panic swept through her that Kristie might be dead.

Still standing on the hood of the Plymouth, she leaned over and tapped a police officer on the shoulder. "How many people are hurt? Do you know any names?"

The cop spit into the street. "No, ma'am. Don't know much right now."

"Do they think there's another bomb?"

"Don't know that either, ma'am."

Suddenly, Sara spotted Rick. He was standing right at the front entrance! She waved her arms and yelled as loud as she could over the noise. "Rick! Rick!" She saw him turn, saw the puzzled look on his face and yelled his name again. Finally, he saw her and started to run.

"Sara!" He slipped underneath the yellow tape, approached the car and lifted her down. "Oh, my God, Sara. Can you believe it? Someone bombed our club."

Sara looked up at him. He'd been crying and his face was smudged with dirt. "Where's Kris?"

"Inside. They're just getting ready to bring her out."

"Is she . . ."

"She's hurt. I don't know how bad." He gestured wildly back toward the club. "The bomb exploded just off The Patio. It was about ten o'clock. She was standing near the bar, a few feet from the door to The Patio." Rick rubbed his eyes. "I saw this weird flash. Then this incredible noise. People were screaming, shoving one another. The lights went out and then flashed back on. Everyone started to push for the exits. It was just awful!"

"I've got to get in there."

"There are still some customers in there, Sara. The police are doing a lousy job. The place should have been totally evacuated long ago."

"Get me in there — I don't care how you do it."

"We'll go up the street and around the back. Take the alley to the rear exit."

Rick grabbed her by the arm and off they ran, behind the Denny's restaurant, through the parking lot to the back alley which was dark and quiet compared to the circus in front of the building. As they got closer, Sara noticed a burning chemical smell that made her feel sick. She and Rick actually got to the back door without being intercepted.

"Hey, what do you think you're doing?" A cop was standing just inside the back entrance. He moved his stocky frame to block them from going any farther.

Rick pulled out his ID. "I work here. So does she."

Before the cop could say anything, Rick yanked her into the hallway that ran behind the small stage, just off the dance floor. Rick parted the long black curtains draping the stage and they stepped out onto the dance floor. The scene was frightening. People in uniform were everywhere: police, paramedics, firefighters.

Sara darted toward what was left of The Patio. The double doors were blown off and the roof had collapsed. Shrapnel, in the form of nails, was everywhere. Sticking in the walls, the floor, the bar and in the people lying all over the floor just to the right of The Patio exit. Sara scanned the prone bodies for Kristie. She found her as they were lifting her onto a gurney.

"Kris, it's Sara. Are you all right?"

Kristie looked up and smiled weakly. One arm was bandaged from shoulder to hand. Her face was pitted and bruised. There were scorch marks on her forehead. "Hey, baby. What brings you out on a night like this?"

"You. I love you, Kris. I'll ride with you to the hospital."

"Okay. Follow me to my own special limo."

Sara walked beside the gurney and followed it to the ambulance. Kristie's eyes were half-closed, but she squeezed Sara's hand hard. "I'm okay. Don't worry."

"Shh. You rest now."

Sara spent the next two hours pacing in the Grady Hospital emergency waiting room. Many of Kristie's friends were there, along with the families of the other victims. The place was chaotic. Nurses, orderlies and doctors ran through the halls. Occasionally, a family member was summoned by hospital personnel.

Rick and Sara held hands. Rick cried like a baby and Sara was starting to worry about him. She held him and rocked him, hoping they would hear something soon.

Eventually, a young surgeon came into the waiting room and asked for "Ms. Trevor's family." Sara and Rick stood up, anxious for any news.

"Her arm was pretty mangled by the shrapnel. But we've repaired most of the damage and with some rehab she should be just fine." The surgeon grabbed his beeper as it went off. "We're going to keep her a few days until the danger of infection has passed. And until we can get some rehab set-up for her."

"What room's she in?" Sara asked.

"She's still in the recovery room. They probably won't move her into a regular room until morning."

Sara and Rick thanked the young doctor. Then Sara made a quick call to work, leaving a message for Natalie that she wouldn't be in until that afternoon. Sara then returned to the waiting room, where she and Rick crashed from exhaustion.

Later that morning, Sara woke up. Rick had left a note that he'd gone home. She reached for the copy of the *Atlanta Journal Constitution,* which someone had left on one of the waiting room chairs. The bombing at Kristie's club was the lead story.

> A bomb exploded last night at a popular lesbian nightclub, injuring at least twenty people. Having received a report that a shooting had occurred at the nightclub, Lavender Nights, located in the popular midtown area of the city, members of the Atlanta SWAT team were dispatched to the scene. They soon spotted a suspicious-looking backpack outside the nightclub in a nearby parking lot. The city bomb squad discovered a second device inside the bag and, after midnight, used a robot to carry out a controlled detonation.

Sara couldn't believe what she was reading. There had actually been two bombs—one that exploded just off The Patio and one in a nearby parking lot that police found before it had time to explode. She finished reading the article.

> Of the twenty people injured in the nightclub explosion, twelve required hospitalization. One of those hospitalized, reportedly, is the owner of the nightclub.
>
> Nightclub patrons claimed to have seen a flash followed by a blast. They described the blast

as resembling an exploding electrical transformer. Several local news reports said the bomb was apparently packed with nails and quoted eyewitnesses saying that some of the victims had nails sticking out of their arms.

The nail-packed device exploded in a rear patio crowded with about 150 people. The most seriously injured was the nightclub's owner who had three- to four-inch nail spikes in her arm. She is listed in stable condition after surgery at Grady Memorial Hospital.

"Several customers thought the owner of the club had been shot," said Rick Stevens, who was tending bar when he saw a flash of light and heard the blast. "We rolled up one of her sleeves and saw she had these horrible spike nails through her arm. Then, we made her lie down on the floor until help came."

Officials believe that the second device may have been placed outside the nightclub in an apparent attempt to injure police and rescue workers responding to the initial emergency call. Police closed off traffic to a three-block, mostly commercial area of restaurants, nightclubs and businesses before exploding the second, more powerful bomb, authorities said.

A federal task force will take over the investigation of the bombing, along with a Bureau of Alcohol, Tobacco and Firearms team that will arrive tomorrow from Washington, D.C. to assist.

Sara folded the newspaper and tucked it under her arm. She got up and stretched out the crick in her neck and the stiffness in her back. Walking down the adjacent corridor, she took the first left. She dug through her pockets for some loose change and bought a cup of coffee and a stale raspberry Danish from a vending machine. Cup of coffee and Danish in hand, she headed for the nurses' station at the end of the hall. Seeing it brought flashbacks of another hospital not so many weeks ago. The pain of saying good-bye to her mother during trip after trip to Pennsylvania was still palpable. The death of her mother had left her with a broken heart—and living with that broken heart was an agonizing adjustment. Physiologically, a broken heart beat just the same, she learned, but the emotions connected to the life it pumped through her were dulled and jaded. She shuddered to think that a heart already broken could have been damaged yet again. Kristie was almost killed. Today Sara might have awakened to the horrible reality that the two women she loved most in the world were dead — a reality she didn't think she could have survived. She thanked God again and again for not giving her the experience.

A nurse at the desk directed her to Kristie's room. Sara sat down in the chair next to the bed. Kristie was asleep. There was an I.V. drip in her left arm and oxygen tubes around her face. The sun was warm through the window behind her, but the room was cool. Through tears she could no longer suppress, she watched Kristie breathe, held her hand, kissed her cheek. She laid her head on the thin, white sheet that covered her friend. And right before a deep sleep came to calm her, she cried and prayed she'd never have to see the inside of another hospital room.

Chapter Eight

The week after the bombing, Sara sat in front of her computer, which was misbehaving. The screen was frozen. Sara clicked the mouse on the "close" program option and nothing happened. Then she pressed the Ctrl-Alt-Delete keys simultaneously and still nothing happened. Exasperated, she shut down the computer.

"That's not good for your hard drive," the voice behind her said. She swung her chair around. It was Paul.

"I know, I know. But the darned thing froze up on me again."

"You should have someone look at it."

Sara laughed nervously. "I will—as soon as I have time for it not to work."

Paul smiled and sat down. "You're working yourself into exhaustion, but I'm about to change all that."

"Really? I'd like to know how."

Paul crossed his legs and folded his hands on top of his knee. For once, he wasn't tugging at his earlobe. In fact, he looked downright serene, oddly calm compared to his recent demeanor. After Sara had refused to give in on the Kodak matter, Paul had snubbed her at every turn, even refusing on most days to say good morning.

"I'm going to give you the break you need, Sara. I'm going to do the Kodak presentation next month."

Sara dropped her pen. She heard it hit the floor and roll. Then she laughed. "No time for jokes, Paul. Time is running short."

"I'm not joking. In fact, I'm quite serious."

Sensing trouble, Sara got up and closed the door. When she sat back down, she said, "Paul you're in no position to be telling me what you're going to do. We've already discussed this and the decision I've made is final."

"I don't think so."

Sara took a deep breath.

"You don't understand. I'm going to make the presentation as a favor to you. In lieu of your losing your job." He flashed a smug smile while smoothing out his tie.

Sara paused, making sure of what she had just heard. "Excuse me?"

"You're going to announce to everyone at the staff meeting this afternoon that I'm making the presentation to Kodak. By doing this, I won't have to expose you to the home office and you won't lose your job."

"Let me get this straight. You're blackmailing me?"

"No, I'm trying to save you your job. You should be a little more appreciative, Sara."

Sara felt a pulsating at the back of her head, her blood pressure soaring. "And just what do you mean by 'expose'?"

Paul replied coldly, "You've got some serious personal problems that, in my opinion, have affected and are still affecting your ability to do your job. I don't believe you can handle the pressure associated with a big account like Kodak. I think you'll crack."

"You think wrong." Sara picked up a stack of files. "These files represent an entire year's work, Paul. It's because of me, and the rest of this staff who've worked their butts off, that we even have a shot at this account."

"Listen, it's quite simple, Sara. If you don't make the announcement to the staff this afternoon, I'm going to fly out to the home office and have a personal meeting with Richard Sanders." Paul pointed to his watch. "The meeting's already set up for tomorrow at four p.m. at the San Francisco home office. I can cancel it, but that's entirely up to you."

"I have no intention of making any such announcement to the staff," Sara snapped. "The strategy direction for the Kodak account is unchanged. I will be making the major portion of the presentation next month, backed up by the key creative people who have already been selected to accompany me."

"You're making a big mistake."

"I don't think so, Paul. I believe you're the one who's making a mistake—no matter how this matter is resolved."

He shrugged nonchalantly. "Okay, suit yourself. I've got some materials to prepare for Sanders, then. Obviously, I won't be in the office tomorrow."

"I won't expect you."

She watched him leave and went back to her work — or at least she tried. Should she call Sanders, she wondered? Or let the chips fall where they may? Clearly, Sanders was still backing his brother-in-law to some degree. But Sanders had passed Paul over for the promotion and had hired Sara after expressing a great deal of confidence in her abilities. Sanders was impressed with the aggressiveness she had demonstrated while attempting to win an audience with Kodak. The date for the pitch was set and she was responsible for creating that opportunity. She would wait. Maybe, just maybe, Paul would put the noose around his own neck.

That evening, she drove directly from work to Grady Hospital. It had gotten to the point where even the sight of a hospital made her queasy.

"How are you?"

Kristie was sitting up in bed. "Hi, sweetie. Much better, thanks. Especially now that you're here."

Sara placed a bouquet of flowers among the ten other arrangements occupying space throughout the room. She sat down on the edge of the bed.

"I love you."

"Love you, too. Thanks for the beautiful flowers."

"You're more than welcome. Any more news from the FBI? Do they know who did this yet?"

"They got a letter from a group claiming responsibility. Some FBI folk were here this morning to interview me again. The agent in charge of the case left a copy of the letter. Hang on a sec and I'll read it to you." Kristie grabbed a single sheet of paper from her night stand. "Wait'll you hear this. 'The attack in midtown was aimed at the sodomite bar, Lavender Nights. We will continue to target sodomites, their organizations and all those who push their agenda. Death to the new world order.' It's signed by a group called the Army of God." Kristie flashed a look of disgust at Sara. "Can you believe that crap?"

Sara took the sheet of paper and read the message again. "Unfortunately, I can. Just what we need in this country — another hate group with the goal of hurting innocent people."

Kristie picked up another pile of papers. "I just hope my insurance will cover all of this," she said, flipping through the stack. "I had Jennifer dig these out for me."

"Won't it?"

"Don't know yet. Terrorism isn't exactly spelled out in the policy. My stupidity, I guess." Kristie waved the insurance papers in the air. "'Course, it wasn't like it hadn't ever crossed my mind." She smacked her forehead with her good hand. "Knew a bomb was always a potential threat. Had enough bomb threats called in over the years. But that's all they were. Threats. Never actually believed someone would follow through on something like this."

Sara ran her fingers through Kristie's hair. "Try not to worry. You'll get it straightened out. First, you need to get better."

Kristie crumpled up the hate letter and threw it across the room. "Sara, I'm going to lose money every day that place is closed. May damned well lose everything."

"No, you won't. We won't let that happen. Have you called Rick?"

"Yeah. He's gonna try to get the place open by the end of the week. The ATF and FBI said they should be done sifting through the mess today. Tomorrow, the cleanup can get started."

"Tell you what. I'll go check on the place for you. See if everything's being handled okay."

Kristie shook her head. "You don't have time for that. Not with this Kodak thing coming up."

Sara quickly debated whether or not to tell Kristie about the most recent developments with Paul. "Well, just like you, I'm not sure what's going to happen with that. Paul's causing problems again — making threats. I don't have a good feeling about it."

"Damn! Everything's fucked up right now." Kristie tried to reposition her arm and winced. "I'm so sorry. Forget about the club. You've got enough to worry about."

Sara moved to the other side of the bed and helped Kristie prop her arm on a pillow. "I'll go check on the club. After work tomorrow, I'll stop by. Do you have the key?"

"In my jacket pocket over there. In that closet."

Sara leaned forward and kissed Kristie's forehead. "I love you, Kris."

"Love you, too." Kristie held her hand. "Listen, that nice woman you've been dating. Jasmin?"

"Yes."

"How're things going with that?"

Sara put her hands on her hips. "Fine. Why?"

"Just wondered. Been thinking a lot about you. How you deserve to start a new life, meet new people. Date pretty women. I know we've talked about our feelings for each other — never really decided on anything for sure. But look at me, Sara. My life's a screwed-up mess." Kristie lay back on the pillow. "Besides, I don't ever want to lose you."

"Lose me?"

"Yeah. Friends are for life, ya know?"

"And lovers aren't?"

"Not in my experience."

"Funny. Not in mine either." Sara laughed. "Besides, I'm not sure I could stand to be dumped by my best friend."

"I would never do such a thing."

"Yes you would. You'd just come up with some real smooth excuse. Like . . . " Sara rolled her eyes and said demurely, "I no longer want to subject you to the pain of my past."

Kristie chuckled. "See, you'll never have to put up with hearing that crap from me."

"I can't say that I'm sorry."

* * * * *

The next day after work, Sara found the entrance to Kristie's club still surrounded by yellow police tape. She ducked underneath the plastic tape and crossed the parking lot. Pulling at the front door, she found that it was open.

Once inside, she could still smell the chemicals that must have been used to ignite the bomb. The place was dark, except for some spotlights turned on over the dance floor. She walked around the bar in the direction of The Patio. The ceiling in front of The Patio was gone — baring piping, electrical wiring and insulation. Large nail spikes were still imbedded in the walls.

She found Rick and some other men cleaning up the leftover debris on The Patio. A truck was parked in the rear lot to haul the mess away.

"Hey, gorgeous!" Rick called.

"Hi, Rick. How's it going?"

"Actually, it's going okay. I got some people coming in tomorrow to fix the ceiling out front. And once we have this mess cleaned up, we can just close off The Patio until it's repaired. May take a few months, but the rest of the place is fine."

"Then you can open this weekend?"

"I don't see why not." He continued to throw charred ceiling tiles into a large plastic bin. "This morning, a crew from the city inspector's office was here to check out the building. Structurally, it really didn't sustain any damage. Since The Patio was an add-on anyway, it just sort of blew apart from everything else."

"That's good news."

“It is.” Rick took off his work gloves and wiped the sweat from his face with the back of his hand. “How’s Kristie? Just talked to her on the phone but haven’t had a chance to get back to the hospital. Figure I can be more help here.”

“She’s doing well, and I know she appreciates all the extra work you’re taking care of here.”

“Listen, if it weren’t for Kristie, I’d probably be dead. I’d do anything for her.”

Sara nodded. Rick had been an addict. Cocaine mostly. One day, he came into the club looking for a job. Kristie said she’d give him one if he got himself cleaned up. She sent him to a friend of hers who ran a drug clinic downtown. As soon as Rick enrolled in the program, she kept her promise and gave him a job. As far as Sara knew, he hadn’t touched drugs since — and that was over a year ago.

Sara took off her suit jacket. “Let me help you here. I have some time to kill.”

Rick grabbed her gently by the arm. “No, honey. You’ll ruin your clothes.”

“Kris has an old coat in her office. I’ll throw that on.”

For the next three hours Sara helped load the truck with the charred remains of The Patio. While she worked, wiping the sweat from her own face, she remembered all too well that if it hadn’t been for Kristie, she might be dead, too.

The rest of the week, the cleanup at Kristie’s club went slowly. Nonstop rain drenched the entire Atlanta area. When the sun finally cleared on Saturday afternoon, Sara couldn't stand to sit in the house any longer. She called Jasmin.

As a result of the weather, the Chattahoochee River ran high along its banks. Sunlit and crowded with people, children and pets, the trail followed the flat river basin to several cut-off paths — and eventually to a park with pavilions.

"This path is a really pretty one," Jasmin said, pointing off to the left. She was wearing khaki camp shorts and an Atlanta Braves T-shirt. She held Sara's hand as they turned onto the path, oblivious to the fact that there were other people around.

Sara smiled. It was the first time in days she felt like it. "It's really beautiful back here."

A dirt path soon became a trail of planked boards raised from a swamp below. The trail reminded Sara of pictures she had seen of the Florida Everglades. Tangled trees hung over the green-tinged water. Dead wood and aquatic plants mingled together, blanketing the swamp in hues of brown, gray and green.

Not far from the main trail was a deck area that extended over the water with wooden benches. Sara and Jasmin sat down in a shaded area to rest. The water hummed with insects. Large dragonflies buzzed and swooped, and bullfrogs jumped, leaving ripples in the water.

"This is an amazing place," Sara said. "I've never been on this part of the trail before."

"It's another one of my favorite spots. I told you I planned to take you to all of them."

"Thank you."

"Do you know what I like about you, Sara?"

Sara took off her sunglasses. "What?"

Jasmin laughed. "I have a whole long list. But I can give you the condensed version."

"Since I don't handle compliments very well, maybe the condensed version would be better."

"I admire your courage and calm, despite everything you've been through." Jasmin took Sara's hand and cupped it between her own. "I also admire your hesitancy — believe it or not — to get involved with someone right now. The fact that you're doing what you need to do for you."

Sara looked out over the water. "You're not helping my hesitancy one bit, Jasmin. I can tell you that." Sara turned back with a smile. "But thank you for understanding."

"You're very important to me. I hope you know that."

"I'm beginning to. And that's a big step for me."

"I know."

"How's Kristie? I talked to her briefly by phone on Friday. Is she feeling better?"

"I think so. Lots of problems with the club, though."

"That's a shame. What happened at Kristie's club is a painful reminder that discrimination is alive and well, whether it's related to race, gender or sexual preference."

"It's sickening."

"Give her my best when you see her."

"I will."

Jasmin rested her head on Sara's shoulder and, together, they watched the afternoon fade to dusk.

* * * * *

Sara now referred to her daily work life as "the countdown to Kodak." Everything she did — every decision she made, meeting she held, phone call she took — was in some way related to the Kodak pitch, which was now only three weeks away.

She had barely spoken to Paul in the past week but he seemed cockier than ever. She had made several attempts to find out what had happened during Paul's visit to the home office in San Francisco. But Paul wasn't cooperating and Sanders was in Europe, visiting a satellite office in London.

Her fingers sped over the computer keys. In the back of her mind, she heard the phones ringing. She knew Bill was pacing outside her office, waiting to see her about the Kodak direct-mail campaign. And Natalie was supposed to be bringing her a fax from Derek Edmonds. Where was she?

As if reading her mind, Natalie appeared. "Sara, here's that fax. Also, Richard Sanders is on the phone. He says it's important."

Sara jumped. "Oh, you startled me."

"Sorry. I did knock."

"That's okay. I was just thinking about you and the fax. Suddenly, you're standing here. Which line is Sanders on?"

"Three."

"Thanks, Natalie. Please tell Bill he'll have to wait a few more minutes."

Natalie glanced in Bill's direction. "Well, okay. But I hope he doesn't have a nervous breakdown."

Sara laughed and then punched line three. "Richard, how are you? Sorry to keep you waiting."

"No problem. Listen, I need to talk with you

about Kodak." He sounded grave. She held her breath.

"Okay."

"When the presentation is made I intend to be there, as you know."

Sara fiddled nervously with the phone cord. "Yes, of course. I believe your presence in Rochester's very important."

"Thank you." There was a pause on the line. "I understand, from our previous discussions, that you'll be making the presentation."

"Yes, the main portion of it. I'll be supported by the creative staff, of course."

"Certainly."

"That's been the plan all along. Preparations are well underway and we're more than ready to give a dynamite creative and strategic pitch."

"I'm sure of that, Sara. But I'm afraid I'm going to have to make a change."

"What do you mean?"

"I'd like Paul to direct the main portion of the presentation."

Sara almost dropped the phone. She paused to catch her breath. "But why, Richard? It's so late in the game. I'm sorry, but this is extremely unwise. I've been personally preparing this presentation for months. I know this account inside and out."

"Yes, and you'll be there to back up the team. But I want Paul to have a major presence." Sanders' tone was emphatic. "He's a key person in our operation there. Second in command. He needs to have more involvement."

Sara leaned forward and supported her head in her hand. "Then let him attend the meeting, Richard.

And let him back up the team. He's been kept in the loop on this pitch from day one. But I've developed the alliance with Kodak. They're going to be looking for me to play the major role."

"I'm afraid my mind is made up. I expect you to support Paul on this — and give him full authority on the decision-making processes as we move into these last weeks."

"If that's your final decision, Richard, then I'll certainly abide by it. Partners Three is your company and you have the ultimate authority."

"Thank you, Sara. I look forward to seeing you in Rochester."

"Yes, of course. Good-bye."

Sara hung up the phone and dropped her head into her hands. It felt like the final stinging blow. She tried to get up from her desk, to collect herself enough to make it to her car. But her brain was numb and the rest of her body wasn't taking orders. So she sat and listened to the phone ring, to the voices in the hall, to the humming of the copier in the next room. She sat and listened to the voices in her head telling her that the last piece of who she was had just been taken.

Chapter Nine

The Tuesday night circle had grown by one. It was always growing. Sad, but true, Sara thought. More women joined and the other women stayed until a circle of twenty gray metal chairs spread outward, consuming the room.

The new woman, Cindy, seemed anxious to share her story, as if she'd been saving it up for years. Sara was struck by her beauty. She was more than attractive. Her deep blue eyes were a contrast to her pale skin and long, brown hair. She was all curves from neck to thigh — curves that filled out her white suit and black satin blouse.

"The first time she hit me was on vacation. We'd saved up our money and gone to San Juan." Cindy looked around the room and shrugged helplessly. "That became a pattern, you know. Ruined vacations, holidays, birthdays. She hated everything about me — at least it seemed that way. My house, dog, job, friends." She laughed sarcastically. "Friends. Pretty soon I didn't have a friend left. She alienated all of them. Thought I was sleeping with them. Actually, she was the one who was sleeping around — with anyone and everyone. Of course, that was okay."

"But of course," Vanessa said in agreement. "That's always okay."

"I tried separating from her for a while," Cindy continued. "But she'd see me dating other women and pursue me until I came back. Until I was stupid enough to go back."

"Don't feel bad," Karen said, blowing a stream of smoke into the circle. "We've all done that."

Cindy smiled. "You know, I only ever defended myself once. She was about to hit me in the face, and I raised my arm to block the blow. She started screaming at me about how violent I was." She closed her eyes and a tear fell. "That night," she said between gasps, "I slept on the couch until she came storming out of the bedroom and started shoving me around again. She eventually shoved me into the bedroom where she tied my wrists to the headboard and forced herself on me." Cindy bowed her head. "She raped me and it was so humiliating. This was someone I had once loved and trusted. That was it.

Finally, I told her it was over. I told her no contact, nothing. That was six months ago, and I'm still looking over my shoulder."

"Just remember you're not alone. All of the women here have had similar experiences," Dr. Langford said in a comforting tone. "We're here to help you rebuild your life and learn that you never have to be a victim of abuse again."

After a long discussion about domestic violence and rape, Dr. Langford moved to end the meeting. "By the way, I want to remind all of you about the dinner being sponsored by Women in Partnership to Stop Lesbian Domestic Violence, the same organization that sponsors this group. The dinner's being held the last Friday in July." Dr. Langford passed a pile of papers to her left and right. "The cost is fifteen dollars. If anyone has a problem with that, please see me after the meeting. I've also been asked to recruit a volunteer to speak at the dinner about the issues you've all expressed here, have experienced and are facing on a day-to-day basis. Please think about it, and let me know if any of you have a desire to talk." Consulting a piece of paper, Dr. Langford adjusted her glasses. "The other keynote speaker will be Dr. Janet Simons, Director of the National Women Against Domestic Violence coalition. I hope you can all be there."

Sara quickly gathered her blazer and briefcase. As she approached the heavy double doors to leave the room, she stopped abruptly. Instinctively, she knew that it was something she needed to do — for herself and for all of them.

She turned and walked back toward the doctor. "Dr. Langford."

"Yes, Sara?"

"I'd like to speak at the dinner," she said matter-of-factly.

The doctor smiled. "I was hoping you would, Sara. Will you need any help preparing your remarks?"

"Just with some background research. If you don't mind."

"Not at all. Stop by my office next week. Say, Wednesday evening around eight?"

"That would be fine. Thank you."

Being at work had always been her escape. Not anymore. As she passed along the rows of cubicles, she felt the stares. Helpless, please-help-us stares that caused tiny beads of sweat to pop out on her forehead. Everyone had been devastated by the news that Paul would be giving the Kodak pitch the following Monday — everyone but Paul. No one had said anything to her. No one had to. The blank stares and smiles that said, "I'm so sorry" had been enough.

In the meantime, Paul had been badgering everyone. There was a palpable tension in the air that had never existed. Everyone looked and acted miserable; the joy in all their efforts to win Kodak seemed to have evaporated overnight. And with that joy and enthusiasm went the Kodak account, Sara thought. They could never pull it off now.

Sara sat down at her desk and sifted through her in-basket. She ignored the ringing phone. What did it matter?

"Hi. Hope I'm not disturbing you."

It was Natalie, standing in her doorway. "No, of course not. Someone important on the phone?"

"Well, here are all your messages. You've had a lot of calls. Some of the messages Toni took." Natalie handed her the small mountain of pink slips.

"Guess I better get busy."

Natalie turned and closed the door. "Sara, I'm just a secretary, so I know I'm speaking out of place."

Sara shook her head. "No, you're not."

Natalie stood directly in front of her desk, wringing her hands. "Everyone's really upset, in case you don't know."

"I do know."

"Isn't there anything you can do?"

"I'm afraid not."

"I'd like to punch his lights out, personally," Natalie whispered. "Egomaniac."

Sara chuckled. "I'd like to help you, Natalie. But then we'd both be out of jobs. Don't worry. Everything will work out okay."

"I hope so." Natalie gestured in the direction of Paul's office. "He's been ordering everyone around like he's some kind of general or something. People are getting ready to quit."

"Hmm. Well, we'll see about that. Do me a favor, will you?"

"Sure."

She handed Natalie the pink message slips. "Give these messages to Bill. Have him call all of these people and find out what they want. If he needs me, or if I need to call anyone back personally, I'll be available all afternoon."

"Okay. Anything else?"

"Pray."

Natalie shifted her weight to one foot and bounced nervously. "Heck, I've been doing that."

"Do it some more. For me."

"I will. By the way . . ." Natalie shrugged and bit the end of her pencil. "All these rumors about you. The problems you've had. I just want you to know I don't care. And no one else does either. We're just glad you're okay."

"What rumors?"

"Umm . . . I guess I shouldn't have said anything."

"No, I'm glad you did. Just gives me more ammunition."

Immediately, Sara left her office and entered the main work area. She scanned the line of cubicles until she caught sight of Paul's head sticking up over the wall near Debbie's cubicle at the end of the middle row.

When she approached them, Paul was holding up one of the Kodak TV boards. "This is not what I asked you to do. When are you going to get it together, Deb?"

When Debbie saw her she jumped. Then she gave Sara a please-help-me look and wheeled her chair back a few feet toward her desk.

"Excuse me, Paul. Is there a problem?" Sara asked sternly.

Paul turned and snapped, "Yes, there sure is a problem. If we don't get these TV boards right, there's going to be an even bigger problem."

Sara took the board from Paul and scanned it. "This isn't the TV creative for Kodak. This is something entirely new. What happened to our original concepts?" Sara looked at Debbie. Debbie looked at Paul.

"We're changing direction on it, that's what's happening," Paul said, grabbing the board back. "The original concepts were way off base. But Deb seems to be having some kind of mental block about it." Paul tossed the oversized board up against Deb's cubicle. "Make sure the changes are made to these by tomorrow. We don't have this kind of time to waste."

Paul stomped off. Sara folded her arms in front of her, trying to remain calm.

"He's impossible to work with. I'm sorry, Sara. I don't know how much more I can stand."

"I know."

"The original concepts were so much better. What should I do?"

"Finish these. But when we go to Rochester, bring the original concepts with you, okay?"

"Okay. Whatever you say."

"And hang in there — as a personal favor to me."

"I will." She smiled, relief in her eyes.

Paul was in his office talking on the phone. Sara waited until he hung up the receiver. "Ahh, Sara. What can I do for you?"

Sara walked in and shut the door. "You know, for someone who wants to make a name for himself, you sure are doing just that. I'm not quite certain it's what you had in mind, but congratulations."

"What are you talking about?"

"Morale. The staff. It's at an all-time low."

Paul swiped at the air with his hand. "They're just stressed. We all are. It's normal."

"I think you're wrong, but the project's in your hands now, so I guess I'll keep my advice to myself."

Paul leaned back in his chair. He had that smug look on his face again. The I-beat-you-at-your-own-game look that made Sara almost blind with rage. "No, no. Glad you mentioned it. But trust me. Everything's fine. Next Monday, everyone and everything will be ready."

Sara picked up a thick folder from his desk. "Did you review this material? It's everything I'd prepared for the presentation."

"Yes, of course. I've made some changes here and there. Made some alternate recommendations. But overall, it looked pretty good to me."

"I'm glad you think so."

Paul draped his arm over the back of his chair. "By the way, Sara, no hard feelings, huh?"

Sara looked him straight in the eye. She noticed he was rubbing his earlobe again. "What's the matter, Paul? Getting a little nervous?"

Paul let go of his ear. "Nervous? Of course not. Nothing to be nervous about."

"Well, I'll leave you to your work. I know you've got a lot to do before next Monday."

"Yes. Thanks for stopping by. Have a good day."

"I will." Sara turned to leave, then swung back around. "By the way, if I find out that you were the one who leaked out the rumors about my personal life to the staff, I'll be seeing you in court."

Paul's head snapped up like it was attached to a rubber band. "Rumors? What rumors? I don't know what you're talking about."

"You better not. Have a great day."

That evening after work, Sara pulled in to Kristie's driveway. Three days of newspapers were piled on the front porch and envelopes, sale circulars and magazines were busting out of the mailbox.

Kristie opened the door in her robe. She'd been home from the hospital for two weeks, but had since slipped into a depressed stupor.

"Been busy?" Sara kissed Kristie's cheek and handed her the mail.

"Yeah, trying to salvage a broken-down club."

"You're looking better."

Kristie smiled. It was a rare occurrence these days. "Never looked better yourself. C'mon in."

Kristie's left arm was still in a sling. She moved stiffly as she walked into the living room. Dudley followed them both, panting happily.

Sara put the old newspapers on top of the regular pile near the love seat and followed Kristie into the kitchen. "How are things at the club?" Sara asked.

"Things are coming along." Kristie took two bottles of beer from the refrigerator. "We're not getting the crowds we need. I guess people are still spooked. Who can blame them?"

Sara leaned up against the kitchen counter. "I'm sorry things aren't going well."

"It'll be okay." Kristie opened the dishwasher. As she emptied the kitchen sink of dirty dishes, Dudley stuck his head inside the dishwasher and snuffled and snorted. "Dudley!" She grabbed his collar and pulled his head out of the machine. "I may lose the place anyway. Still fighting with the insurance company. I've already put so much of my own money into the cleanup, I don't know how much more I can invest."

Sara squeezed Kristie's hand. "What can I do?"

"Nothing. Just be here for me, like you have

been." Kristie slammed the dishwasher. "Did you hear that the club bombing may be linked to the Olympic Park bombing?"

"Oh, my God. No, I didn't."

"Yep, and that abortion clinic bombing, too."

"I can't believe it, Kris. That's downright scary."

"To know there's a goddamned mad bomber loose in Atlanta? Hell, yeah. Scares the crap outta me." Kristie looked around the room. "Hey, did ya notice?"

"Notice what?"

"I cleaned. Looks pretty good, don't it?"

Swallowing a sip of beer, Sara rolled her eyes. She looked around the cluttered room, trying to take it all in. The kitchen counter was strewn with stacks of unopened mail, unread magazines and piles of old phone books. Pots were hanging out of the lower cabinet, making it impossible to close the cabinet door. The refrigerator was covered with newspaper clippings, greeting cards, reminder notes, old grocery lists and magazine articles. About a hundred magnets held it all up there. Whenever Sara opened the refrigerator door, something always fell to the floor. Old coffee cups, each with an inch of cold coffee and an accompanying spoon, were on every counter. "Kris, no wonder you live alone. You really sort of need to."

Kristie kicked the cabinet door with the pots hanging out. It still wouldn't close. "You're so damned kind. Why don't you just come right out and say I'm a slob?"

"Because that would be unkind."

"Damn, you're really something. Tell me about you. What's happening at work? I'm assuming Paul is still giving the presentation next week."

Sara looked down at the floor. There were muddy

paw prints leading from the living room into the kitchen. "Yes."

"When are you gonna see a lawyer about all this shit?"

"The week after next. I have to help get the staff through all of this nonsense—and time is short. When all is said and done with Kodak, whatever happens, I definitely need to consult my attorney."

"Yeah, you do." Kristie finished loading the dishwasher. Sara handed her some of the dirty coffee cups. "Thanks."

Sara raised her eyebrows and smiled. "Didn't want you to miss them."

"Smart ass. Hear from Jasmin recently?"

"She calls me twice a week or so. I call her back. We talk. We get together when we can."

Kristie grabbed another beer from the refrigerator. "I'm glad," she said gruffly. "Seems like a really nice person."

"She is. But my main concern right now is you. And my job, which seems to be going straight to hell."

"Hey, I told you," Kristie said, her voice on edge. "I'll be okay. Not even a bomb can stop me." She took a gulp of her beer and dug a dog biscuit out of the open box on the counter. "You gotta do what you gotta do. Especially with the job situation." Dudley snapped up the biscuit and trotted into the living room.

"Whatever's going to happen with the job is going to happen, Kris. I want to help you."

"You've done enough."

"So have you."

"You don't quit, do you?"

Sara took off her suit jacket and hung it over one of the kitchen chairs. "What are you upset about?"

"I'm not upset."

"Okay. We don't have to talk about it."

"Talk about what?"

"Your bad mood."

"I'm not in a bad mood."

"Whatever you say. When's the arm going to be better?"

"Couple of weeks I can take this thing off. Month or two of rehab, then I'll be as good as new."

"I can expect my dance partner will be back, then?"

"If you want her."

"Of course I want her."

Kristie put her good arm around Sara's shoulder. "I'm sorry. I need a hug."

Sara put her arms around Kristie and squeezed gently. "That's never a problem. And there's nothing to be sorry about. You're dealing with a lot right now."

Kristie pulled away and hung her head. "It's not just that."

"What?"

"I'm afraid of losing you." The words were barely audible.

Sara frowned and crossed her arms. "What on earth are you talking about?"

"Well, you've got Jasmin now and . . ."

"Have you lost your fucking mind?"

Kristie looked at her. A few moments passed and then she started to laugh. She bent over double, slapping her knee.

"What's so funny, Miss Thang?"

"I'm sorry, baby." More laughter. "It's just that I hardly ever hear you curse. And you really don't do it all that well."

Sara started laughing. Pretty soon they were both sitting on the floor laughing uncontrollably. Tears streamed down Sara's face. Dudley sat in front of them, his head cocked to one side.

"He thinks we're both crazy," Kristie said in between gasps.

"He's right." Sara held her stomach to keep it from hurting. "Kris, you're never going to lose me, don't you know that?"

"Sorry. Weak moment."

"I love you."

"Love you, too."

Dudley barked.

"Yeah, yeah. We love you, too," Kristie said, pulling Sara closer.

Sara rested her head on Kristie's shoulder. "A jealous friend and her jealous dog. I don't think I can take much more of this."

"You ain't got a choice."

"Tell me about it."

On Wednesday evening, Sara opened the door to Dr. Langford's office, which looked more like the inside of someone's living room. She wasn't quite sure where to sit. Reluctantly, she sat on the sofa just inside the doorway. She was the only person there and the place was oddly quiet except for the ticking of a carriage clock on the mantel across the room. She glanced through an old *People* magazine she snatched from the glass-topped coffee table in front of the sofa.

"Sara, how nice to see you."

Sara looked up from the magazine and did a double take. She almost didn't recognize the doctor. She was dressed in blue jeans and a Georgia State University T-shirt. Her hair was let down over her shoulders, instead of tied back as it normally was. "Hi, Dr. Langford."

"Good evening, Sara. I'm so thrilled you're going to speak at the dinner," she said while picking some dead leaves off of an enormous jade plant. "And I'm glad you stopped by. I've gathered some information for you that I think you'll find extremely helpful when you prepare your remarks."

"Thank you very much for the help."

"My pleasure." The doctor motioned Sara to follow her. "Come join me in the kitchen. Care for a glass of wine?"

"Sure. Thank you."

They turned left down the hall to the kitchen. "Please, sit down." The doctor opened the refrigerator and grabbed a bottle of wine. "How's the job going, Sara?"

"It's having its ups and downs right now."

The doctor pressed the levers of the corkscrew down and the cork popped out. "I'm sorry to hear that."

"It's okay. I'm preparing myself for whatever happens."

"That's wise, I suppose."

The wine tasted okay — not too sweet. Sara knew

nothing about wines and wasn't crazy about any of them. But, by her standards, this one was tolerable. "What kind of wine is this, may I ask?"

The doctor turned the bottle so that the label faced Sara. "It's a Merlot. French."

"It's quite good."

"Glad you like it."

"The discussion group has really helped me a lot. I just wanted to thank you."

"That's nice of you to say. But it's the women in the group who make it work. I'm only the facilitator." The doctor took a sip of her wine. "I was married once, you know."

"Oh no, I didn't."

"Abusive relationship. He nearly killed me. After that, I knew I had to do something, not only for myself, but for other women like me."

"Why lesbians?"

"The issues of violence are the same. That needs to be understood. I'm afraid we have a long road ahead — making people understand that same-sex relationships are also grappling with domestic violence issues." Putting down her glass, she handed Sara a manila file folder. "Here's some information I think will help you frame your talk. If you need anything else, just give me a call."

"Thanks. I appreciate your help."

The doctor stopped as though she heard something. "Hold on one second, Sara. Do you mind?"

"No, not at all."

The doctor left the room. Sara drank her wine and studied the kitchen. It was a chef's kitchen or at least the kitchen of someone who liked to cook.

Everything was conveniently organized. The range was a professional-style natural gas model with high-powered burners. The central island also had a gas cooktop, and assorted pots and pans of every size hung overhead. The cabinets were European style — white and seamless. Kohler faucets, Corian countertops, expensive vinyl flooring. It was a beautiful room, but also extremely functional.

"Sara, this is Sandy."

Sara got up and shook the woman's hand. She was tall and lean with auburn hair and hazel eyes — eyes that reminded her of her mother's.

"Hi, Sara. Nice to meet you." Sandy leaned against the Sub-zero refrigerator. "I understand you're giving a talk for Helen about domestic violence."

"Yes, that's right."

Sandy was dressed in a white jacket, pink satin shell and blue jeans. "Important topic. Good luck."

"Thanks."

"Say, I'd love to sit and have a glass of wine with you guys, but I'm preparing a lecture for my next law class."

"Oh, I understand," Sara said. "I'm glad you took the time to say hello."

"Will you come back and join us for dinner sometime? Helen's a dynamite cook."

"I'd love to. Thanks."

"Great. See you again, then."

The doctor sat back down and swirled the wine in her glass. "Sandy and I have been together for three years. She teaches law at G.S.U."

"She seems incredibly nice."

"She is."

"Thank you for introducing us."

"My pleasure." The doctor held up her wine glass. "Well, Sara. Here's to your speech. I'm looking forward to it and I'm very grateful you volunteered."

"It's something I really want to do."

The two glasses clinked together.

"You've come a long way, Sara."

"I know. And I'm finally able to feel it."

Chapter Ten

It was a gorgeous sunny Saturday. After a lot of work, the flower beds outside Jasmin's house were finally free of weeds. The pansies, begonia, petunias and impatiens would spread much better now. Sara patted the last bit of earth smooth around the beds and scooted back to take a look. The entire front of the house was a blanket of purple, yellow, white, and blue flowers — minus the flower-choking weeds.

"God, it looks gorgeous," Sara exclaimed.

"So do you," Jasmin said, stooping down next to her. "Thanks for your help."

"Oh, no problem. When I lived in Pennsylvania and had my own home, flower gardening was my favorite thing to do. Something I inherited from my mom." Sara chuckled. "Weeds are a bad thing, Jasmin. They tend to kill the flowers."

"I know. I've neglected the yard lately. Too busy. But I do appreciate your help."

"You're welcome. Once we spread the mulch, it'll help keep the weeds away."

"Take a break?"

Sara removed her work gloves and stood up. "Good idea. We still have the side yard and back to do."

Jasmin laughed. "We don't have to do it all in one day. Besides, that means you'll have to visit again."

"Ahh, an ulterior motive."

"Of course."

The deck extended from the rear entrance into the fenced-in yard. Jasmin and Sara sat on a built-in bench sipping sweet tea. There was a beautiful hammock hung between two oak trees near the back rail fence.

"Now that looks comfortable," Sara said, pointing to the hammock.

"Want to try it out?"

"Sure do."

Less than a minute later, Sara swung peacefully between the two trees. When she looked up all she saw were leaves and the blue, cloudless sky. Then, she saw Jasmin leaning over her.

"Comfortable?"

"I most certainly am. Care to join me?"

"Would love to."

They lay side-by-side. Sara put her arm behind Jasmin's back and closed her eyes. She was sure that at any second, she could fall asleep. The sun felt soothing on her face and a light breeze blew through the trees. Just when she thought she might drift off, she felt the soft pressure of lips against her own.

"Hello!" Sara opened her eyes.

Jasmin smiled. "Sorry. Couldn't resist. You looked so beautiful lying there, and you were much too close in proximity for me to pass up the opportunity."

"Oh, really?"

"Yes, really."

"Hmm. I can't say that it wasn't nice."

"I hope not." Jasmin rolled over on top of Sara. "Because I plan to do it again."

Jasmin's movement caused the hammock to swing and Sara placed one hand on the ground to brace them. The second kiss was just as soft, but more intimate than the first, long and deep enough to make Sara's heart flutter. Sara lifted her hand from the ground to touch Jasmin's face. She looked into those irresistible brown eyes and, for a moment, was completely lost to the place or time. She couldn't explain the evolution of her feelings for this woman. There was something so disarming about Jasmin, so comfortable. She wanted so much to feel again. If she could only let go . . .

Jasmin leaned into another kiss. The shift of weight swung the hammock over. Sara's next view was the bottom side of the hammock from the ground.

Jasmin landed about a foot away. She started to laugh and crawled toward Sara. "I'm so sorry," she said, holding her sides. "Are you all right."

"Oh, some minor spinal damage, partial paralysis, mild concussion. But the kiss was sure worth it."

They both started to laugh. Sara reached out and took Jasmin's hand to pull her closer. "How 'bout we try that again at ground level."

"My pleasure."

The "countdown to Kodak" was officially down to zero. The small auditorium was filled with Kodak marketing and communications representatives and the staff members of Partners Three who had gathered to make the agency's formal presentation. A table had been setup in the front of the room, panel-style. Sara's staff had already completed arranging their equipment. Donna Price, broadcast production supervisor, sat to her far right. Jason Allen, consumer marketing coordinator, sat to her immediate right. Debbie Bailey, art director, was to her left, and Bill McCall, creative director, was to her far left. She watched as Bill pushed the button on the wall to lower the projection screen. Paul was to Bill's left, squinting at the laptop that stored the PowerPoint presentation.

In the audience was Derek Edmonds of Kodak, accompanied by eight of the major players on his staff. Also, sitting to Edmonds' immediate right, was Richard Sanders. Earlier, Sara had run into Sanders in the hallway outside the room. He smiled warmly but avoided conversation — rushing into the auditorium to find a seat.

There was a heaviness in Sara's chest as she waited for the meeting to begin. All the months of work and meetings and conference calls and research marathons had come down to this moment. Instead of rejoicing in the culmination of all of that work, she saw the moment as a disappointment and an end to her work for Partners Three.

Paul cleared his throat and began to speak. Sara noticed that he seemed extremely nervous. He was doing the earlobe thing, and his voice cracked when he spoke. An awful feeling began to creep into the pit of her stomach. She reached for her water glass and drank half of it.

"Thank you for giving us the opportunity to speak to you today," Paul said. "Partners Three has prepared for Kodak a comprehensive—" Paul stopped in the middle of the sentence. He fumbled with his notes, trying to find his place. "Excuse me," he said, looking up. "A comprehensive creative and strategy proposal that will pave the way for your leadership in the consumer camera market well into the next millennium." Paul looked up, then back down at his notes.

A few moments passed. Moments that seemed like years. Everyone at the Partners Three table was squirming uncomfortably in their seats.

"Well, let me show you some interesting research statistics, relative to your market," Paul finally said. He sidestepped toward the laptop. The mouse pointer bounced wildly across the screen. Finally, he was able to click on the arrow and the first slide was displayed. "Let me first talk about strategy." He squinted at the slide and glanced back at his notes. "Make that creative." He smiled weakly. "Let me first talk about creative and the marketing reasons behind the creative approach we've taken."

"What the hell's wrong with him?" Jason whispered into her ear.

Sara shrugged. She looked at Richard Sanders. He was clearly in a panic — almost as palpable as Paul's. She could read it in his eyes. She prayed that Paul would settle down — that the nerves would disappear. If not, they were in for a long afternoon. This was not how she wanted to lose Kodak, she thought. She was not the only one who had worked hard. Everyone employed at the agency had spilled blood over this account. And now Paul was cutting their throats for the final blood-letting.

"Let's talk about television and what that medium is going to do for Kodak." Paul fumbled with the laptop, trying to click to the next slide. The computer screen was frozen. Frantically, he punched the keys. The projection screen went suddenly blank. Paul turned toward Bill and said something. Bill got up and worked for a few minutes, trying to salvage the file. Paul stood by, looking helpless.

"Well, that's the end of it all," Jason said under his breath. "He doesn't even know how to work the laptop."

Sara glanced at Sanders. He was staring right at her — a look of utter helplessness plastered across his face. Then he was up from his seat, walking down the aisle to the front of the room.

"I want to thank Paul for doing the initial overview into our creative and strategic planning," Sanders said in a calm, matter-of-fact tone. While Sanders talked, Bill tried rebooting the computer. "Now, I'd like to turn things over to Sara Gray, our executive president of strategic development. Most of you have met Sara, and I know she's looking forward to taking you through the rest of our presentation." Sanders turned toward her. There was a pleading look in his eyes. "Sara?"

Sara smiled and got up. Paul passed her on the way to take her seat. He didn't even look at her. Sweat was pouring down his forehead. He appeared to be in shock and in a hurry to sit down.

She positioned herself next to the computer. Bill leaned over and whispered, "The file's gone. He must've screwed it up while beating on the thing."

So be it, Sara thought. "What a pleasure to have this opportunity," she said, looking out at Edmonds' staff. "I've had the distinct honor of working with many of you as Partners Three went through the process of identifying your company's marketing and strategy goals." Sara walked out in front of the table and left the computer behind. She knew the information by heart and instinctively decided at that moment to let the agency's work speak for itself. "We can talk about consumer buying habits and market research and product development all afternoon," she said. "But the bottom line is this: how can Partners Three partner with you to make your product the consumer's number one preference?" Sara turned to her staff. "These are the people at the heart of who we are as an agency and as a company. They've worked hard to develop some refreshing creative concepts and unique marketing strategies we think you'll find to be completely on target. So, let's get right into it. Let us show you what we're proposing and why."

Sara introduced each member of the staff. Then the real show began. Rough-cut television concepts were shown by video, radio advertisements were played by audio, direct-mail campaigns, direct-TV infomercials, print for newspaper and magazine, billboard designs and a host of collateral materials were presented via a computer-to-monitor hookup, which worked flawlessly. Each member of her staff gave a dynamic presentation — filled with the enthusiasm she'd thought was lost. At the end, she shook each of their hands and congratulated them. Whether the agency had won the account or not, it was their work that would be remembered — at least by her.

Afterward, in the hallway outside the auditorium, Richard Sanders approached her. "Well, my lack of judgment may have lost us the account," he said. "But if we are awarded the business, it will be because of you and your wonderful staff. They were brilliant. Really."

"I'm glad you think so."

"As far as your role at the agency is concerned, let me say this —"

"Can we wait to discuss this, Richard? I'd really like to take my staff out for a celebration dinner. They deserve it." Sara looked around at the Kodak staff members still lingering in the hallway. "This may not be the best place to have this conversation anyway."

Sanders scanned the hallway. "No, of course not. I'm just eager to rectify a situation worsened by myself. I'll make arrangements to meet with you early next week."

"Thank you."

"Sara, thank you so much for all the work you've done on Kodak's behalf." It was Derek Edmonds. He was smiling from ear-to-ear. "It was extremely enjoyable. Whatever our decision, please know how personally impressed I am. I'm sure the rest of my staff feels the same way."

"Thank you, Derek. I had a great time working with you. I look forward to speaking with you in the near future."

"Of course. And have a safe trip back to Atlanta."

Edmonds turned and left the area without even speaking to Sanders. It was a rebuff that did not go unnoticed.

"Even Edmonds thinks I'm an idiot." Sanders picked up his briefcase and started down the hall. "From now on I'll stick to mergers and acquisitions. Take care, Sara. See you next week."

"Yes. Next week."

Friday night Kristie was sitting at her desk in the club. It was more cluttered than ever. Stacks and stacks of envelopes were littered from one end of the desk to the other.

"I'm sorry. I didn't realize you were so busy." Sara strolled past Kristie to the photo gallery on the wall. There were new photos. One was from the front page of the newspaper — police cars lining the streets outside the building just after the blast. Others showed the destroyed Patio and investigators sifting through the rubble. "What's new?" Sara asked, staring at the photos, still unable to accept what had happened to the club.

Kristie glanced toward Sara and smiled. "Baby, you wouldn't believe it. See these envelopes?" She passed her hand over the desk. "Donations.

Thousands of dollars. Enough to pay for some of the repairs to the club."

"God, Kris. That's great! But how?"

"Someone got the newspaper to print an article about the club, the bombing and how it's hurt the business. Since the article appeared on Monday, the money's been pouring in every day."

"Save me a copy, okay? Obviously, it didn't appear in the Rochester newspaper."

"I've got extra papers. No problem."

"Here's some more." Rick stepped in between Sara and Kristie, plopping some more envelopes in front of her. "Seems like a lot of people want to help."

"The money will help get The Patio rebuilt, and I'll be able to afford some extra security. I've still got insurance problems," Kristie said, waving some documents in the air. "But one step at a time, I guess."

"I've learned to play by those rules," Rick said. "One day at a time."

Kristie scratched her head. "What I can't understand is who got the paper to print the article."

"Don't know, Kris," Sara said. "You've had a lot of faithful customers over the years."

"For a while, I didn't think anyone cared." Kristie began flipping through the envelopes. "Guess I was wrong."

"Business is picking up again," Rick said. "There's a lot of solidarity in the community about what happened here."

Sara put her arm around Kristie. "I'm so happy for you."

"Thanks, baby." Kristie got up and gave each one

of them a hug. "I couldn't have gotten through this without you guys."

Rick headed toward the door. He held it open for them. "I think a special drink is in order, ladies. Come try my new Blue Moon Punch recipe."

"Blue Moon Punch?" Sara asked. "Good Lord, what's that?"

Kristie laughed. "If Rick invented it, then it's something you'll have only once in a blue moon."

"Precisely," Rick said. "C'mon. It's on the house."

Kristie took Sara's hand. "No wonder I never have any money," she grumbled. "He gives the stuff away."

Now that the drama with Kodak had ended, Sara wondered how the repercussions of that meeting would play out. As she pulled into her parking space Monday morning, she squinted. There was a man standing in front of the building. He was pacing back and forth near the plaza. He stopped briefly to gaze at the fountain, which was surrounded by colorful pansies and begonia. From where she sat, it looked a lot like Richard Sanders.

Lugging her briefcase, newspaper, cup of coffee and laptop, Sara staggered toward the building. It was Richard Sanders. As soon as he saw her, he strode toward her.

"Here, let me help you," he said, taking the laptop and newspaper.

"Thanks. I need someone like you to meet me out front everyday."

Sanders laughed and tucked the newspaper under

his arm. "That's what happens when you take the office home with you as we all seem to do now."

"You're right."

The wind blew Sanders' hair back to expose a receding hairline. "Sara, before we go inside, I'd like to talk with you for a moment."

"Of course." Sara stopped and put her briefcase on the sidewalk. She opened her coffee and took a sip. *What was it now?* she wondered.

"As you know, Paul has been sending me memorandums for quite some time."

"Yes, I know. At least I do now."

Sanders set the laptop case down. "Well, the reason you never heard from me about the memos is because I was shocked at the personal nature of them — and was not about to act on them in any way. Your job performance never warranted any action whatsoever." Clearing his throat, he took her *Wall Street Journal* and began rolling it into a tube. "I think it's remarkable that, under the circumstances you may have been dealing with personally, you were able to do such an outstanding job." Sanders smacked the palm of his hand with the rolled-up newspaper. "I finally demanded that Paul stop sending me memos about you. Told him that he was putting us in line for a lawsuit. He did stop sending them. Then, a couple of months ago, he started calling me. Claimed the entire office was in a shambles. That the Kodak account was in jeopardy. Of course, that's when I visited with you in Rochester."

"I see."

"Didn't find any evidence that anything was wrong."

"Thank you."

The newspaper cracked again. "So, I'm sure you're probably wondering why I selected Paul to give the presentation to Kodak."

"Yes, I am."

"He threatened to send everything he had on you to Derek Edmonds at Kodak. Immediately, I put into motion the steps I needed to take to dismiss him from his job." Sanders shoved his free hand into his trouser pocket. He waved the newspaper with his other hand, as if conducting a symphony. "He is, by the way, no longer with the company."

Sara's head dropped. "Oh, God. I can't believe it."

"He's also going to be prosecuted for attempted blackmail. I'm going to pay all the legal costs myself. But I may need your help."

"Of course, Richard. Whatever you need me to do."

"I would have fired the bastard on the spot." Sanders laughed softly. "Sorry for the language. But I didn't want all the work you had done to be compromised. So I told him to give the presentation. I figured I'd fire him after it was all over. When we had the account or didn't have it. Of course, I didn't count on him to make an ass of himself while actually giving the presentation." Sanders shook his head. "Maybe he knew. The point is, he's history."

"I'm sorry for all of this, Richard."

"No, I'm sorry. I guess my sister's not too happy with me. But I've got a business to run." He smiled and picked up the laptop. "Let's go inside, shall we? I want to make sure you're not history. We need to talk about your future here, if that's all right with you."

Sanders opened the door into the suite. The main reception desk was empty.

"That's odd," Sara said, scanning the immediate area. "I wonder where Toni is."

Sanders shrugged. "I'm sure she's around somewhere."

They took a left past the three-dimensional gold metallic sign and entered the main work area. Suddenly, Sara was blinded by camera flashes. People were clapping and cheering, yelling out her name. Then she saw the banner hanging across the far wall in the main room.

"Congratulations, Sara, our new CEO," the banner proclaimed.

Sara blinked again and again. The entire staff was standing in a group, their arms around one another's shoulders. Streamers hung from the ceiling. A buffet table was covered with bottles of champagne, pastries and fruit.

"We thought you might enjoy a champagne breakfast," Sanders said. He reached over and shook her hand. "This company is in need of its own chief executive officer now. Especially with a new client like Kodak to service."

Sara couldn't speak. They had won the Kodak account? Surely, she was dreaming. "Whatever's going on, I hope I don't wake up from this wonderful dream," she said finally.

"You're not dreaming, Sara." Bill stepped forward and shook her hand. "Congratulations."

Sara felt the tears stinging in her eyes. She reached up and hugged Bill. "Thanks so much." Sara looked out over the rest of the group. "I hope those pictures all of you took earlier were taken with Kodak cameras!"

The group laughed and then, one by one, stepped up and congratulated her. She thanked each one of them for the hard work and extra effort.

"Speech, speech," they yelled, after everyone had spoken to her personally.

"I hardly know what to say, except that what I thought and said all along was right. This is the best group of creative and strategic thinkers in this business." Sara turned to Sanders. "Thank you, Richard, for your support and for this wonderful new opportunity."

"Congratulations, Sara. May I say a few words to the staff?"

"Of course."

Still wielding the *Wall Street Journal*, Sanders spoke with excitement about the future of the company. "Now that the Kodak account's ours, we'll be expanding. We plan to open up satellite offices in several other major cities, including New York to service the Kodak business. The majority of Sara's time will be spent overseeing the growth of the agency."

A round of cheers went up from the staff.

"That means a larger staff and new opportunities for many of you, which Sara will outline over the next few weeks. Now, I'd like to turn it back over to Sara. She's got a little something for each one of you."

Natalie handed Sara a stack of envelopes. "Richard and I had discussed many weeks ago how each one of you would be recognized for your hard work and dedication in achieving the Kodak business. I believe very strongly in employee recognition, no matter what your job or role. And there isn't a single person in this organization who wasn't involved in this victory. Not one." Sara started handing out the envelopes. "Now, it's my turn to say congratulations. Don't spend your bonus checks all in one place."

The group laughed and accepted their checks.

"Let's celebrate," Sara said. "And then we're taking the rest of the day off." Sara turned to Sanders. "And I'll need a new copy of the *Wall Street Journal*. As you can see, Richard has destroyed mine."

Sanders laughed and then escorted her to the buffet table. Opening the first bottle of champagne, he proposed a toast. "To all of you for your hard work and dedication. And to Kodak for making the right choice. No more Fuji film for me," he declared. "As for cameras," he said, taking a sip of champagne, "I guess I better head over to the mall as soon as it opens."

The sounds of laughter were accompanied by the explosions of champagne bottles. Minutes later sprays of champagne filled the air. More photographs were taken. More laughter was heard. And Sara never woke up from the dream of a lifetime.

Chapter Eleven

Still high on the events of that morning, Sara was more than happy to bask in those moments with Jasmin.

"Can you get the rest of the day off?" she asked Jasmin over the phone.

"I think so. Why?"

"Let's go do something fun. I'm in the mood to celebrate."

Sara described to Jasmin what had happened at the office.

"Oh, Sara, that's wonderful! I'm so proud of you. This is definitely cause for celebration."

"I think so."

"What would you like to do?"

"Take me someplace special. Anywhere, so long as I'm with you."

"I know just the place."

As Sara drove to meet Jasmin, she thought about the feelings that were swirling inside of her. Commitment to anyone was frightening. There was still so much pain in her heart. But the tenderness and compassion Jasmin had shown were slowly erasing the doubts she had about letting someone into her life. Kristie had brought her strength and resolve. And she had clung to her friend for support and guidance. Jasmin had shown that understanding and gentleness could actually begin to heal her wounds and restore the trust that had been shattered over a three-year period.

That afternoon Sara and Jasmin headed down International Boulevard to Centennial Olympic Park, which had recently been rededicated and reopened with a grand celebration of music and fireworks. The park, previously remembered only for the tragic bombing which took place there during the Olympic Games, was once again a focal point of the city.

Sara and Jasmin walked leisurely through the park on that warm July day, following the pathways of commemorative brick pavers. Each path led to a memory "quilt" garden that signified a special part of the 1996 games. The first was dedicated to Billy "Porter" Payne, the man credited with bringing the Olympic Games to Atlanta. A bronze statue of Payne dominated this small square, along with quotes from speeches he had made. The next quilt was dedicated to that one shocking evening that took the lives of two people and injured so many others. The date, July 28, 1996, was carved into stone so no one would ever forget the blast that rocked the world, but failed to dispel the spirit of the games. A final quilt honored every athlete who had won a medal and returned home with the symbol of Olympic glory.

Sara and Jasmin sat at the edge of a fountain that cascaded into waterfalls. The park was quiet on this workday afternoon. A few people sunbathed and some pets were being walked. The heat was intense. Sara wiped the perspiration from her forehead.

"What do you think?" Jasmin asked, leaning back against a granite wall.

"Of the park?"

"Yes."

"It's beautiful. The city did a great job. It's a wonderful tribute to the Games."

"I agree." Jasmin took off her sneakers and socks and dangled her feet in the fountain. "I like it when you tell me what you're thinking."

Sara took off her sunglasses. "Oh, really? Why, don't I?"

"Not much."

"I didn't realize that."

"You've had a lot going on in your life. I understand."

Sara moved closer to her. She took off her sneakers and socks, too. The water felt cool in the hot sun. "I'm sorry. There's really a lot I want to say."

Jasmin turned. Her soft, brown skin was also beaded with sweat. "Like what?"

Sara touched Jasmin's cheek with her hand. "I've wanted to say how much you've come to mean to me. How much I care about you." Sara quickly looked away. "But I've been too afraid."

"I care a great deal about you too, Sara."

Sara's head snapped up. "Do you?"

"Very much. Getting to know you has been a wonderful experience, one I've never had before."

"I didn't realize . . ."

"What?"

"That you cared so much." Sara stopped and ran her fingertips through the cool water.

"I do care, Sara. But I know what you've been through, so I've been hesitant to talk about my feelings for you."

Sara leaned back on her hands, kicking the water with her feet. "It'll be a long time before the scars heal, you know."

"I know."

"Will you be patient with me? I'm going to have some bad moments here and there."

Jasmin's voice was reassuring. "I want you to have the time you need to rest and heal. I'll be patient for as long as you need me to be."

"Promise?"

"Promise."

Jasmin took Sara's hand and held it. Neither one of them cared about the stares, if there were any. It was the park and the sun and the water . . . and them. Just them.

* * * * *

A few days later, in the sun-streaked warmth of Jasmin's bedroom, it was just them, too. Intimate moments Sara no longer feared. In the last three months, she had finally learned that caring could be gentle when it was real and mutually felt. Sara's head spun like a top. Jasmin's kisses were soft and passionate, not rough and hurried like the ones she had known. Inside, she trembled at Jasmin's touch, but not from fear.

Jasmin lay on top of her, the warmth of her dark skin melting into her own. She held her close, finally wanting someone more than she wanted to breathe. The ache in her thighs smothered the ache in her heart.

"You're so beautiful," Jasmin said.

Sara could feel her nipples harden with Jasmin's gentle touch, her tongue passing over them lightly enough to tease. Sara arched her back to push them deeper into Jasmin's mouth. She clutched Jasmin's back, damp with perspiration, and held her tight. Running her fingers through Jasmin's short curls, she kissed her forehead again and again.

Jasmin kissed her, then slid her tongue slowly down her abdomen to her inner thigh. Caressed her legs with deep massages, showered her thighs with soft, biting kisses.

The first stroke made her gasp. The next made her move toward the thrust. Slow, deep penetrations made her shudder from head to toe.

Sara gave herself up to Jasmin's touch. She felt everything and let her know it. For the first time in years, she felt a part of someone else. And when Jasmin was inside of her, she rode the loving strokes of a hand that was gentle. The caresses and kisses up and down her body shivered in her spine. She held onto the first orgasm as long as possible, not wanting to lose the moment. When she came she cried out. She felt the orgasm shoot down her thighs and calves to the bottom of her feet. And then the tears fell because it had been real and powerful and shared.

"How lovely you are," Jasmin said.

"You make me feel beautiful. Sexy. I haven't felt that way in a long time."

Minutes later, she was making love to Jasmin. And when Jasmin came, Sara came, too — back to life in that dark, unlit room.

Late at night, during the final weeks before the Kodak pitch, Sara had put her agency work aside. Using notes she had gathered from friends and the information provided by Dr. Langford, she had prepared her talk for the domestic violence awareness dinner.

The banquet hall was filled with about a hundred people, mostly women. As Sara walked up the stage toward the podium, she felt an odd déjà vu that thrust her back to the day of her mother's memorial service. Another speech on a different day that still weighted her heart with sadness. That day, struggling to feel through the pain and the loss, she had not sensed her mother's presence. But on this night, she felt it very strongly, as if her mother were standing right by her side.

Preparing to speak to the crowd, she assumed the

role of advocate proudly. It was a role she knew her mother had experienced so many times during her career as an advocate for the poor, the old, the homeless and hungry, the sick. Standing there, in a position to help others find a better way, humbled her.

Sara finished arranging her notes and looked up. To her right, at a table on the dais was Dr. Helen Langford. In the front row, sitting just below her, was a circle of familiar faces: Kristie, Jasmin, Rick and Richard Sanders. She'd asked them to attend, to be her guests at the table she'd bought. Sanders' presence touched her greatly. All along he had supported her, when she actually thought differently. In a very gratifying way, he had acknowledged her triumph over her personal tragedies by giving her the promotion he knew she deserved.

"I'm honored to be here tonight to share a part of who I am with you. For two years, I was a battered lesbian and lived in fear and apprehension, in hope and in silence. But the time for silence has long passed and I want to share with you what I've learned about myself and about women like myself." Sara adjusted the microphone. She cleared her throat and continued. "Lesbian relationships involving domestic violence are not about two women fighting. These relationships, like any others of their kind, are about violence, power and control. The abuser's goal is to dominate and disempower the victim. It's a cycle of behavior that includes periods of abuse as well as periods of love and calm."

She paused, thinking of Karen, who had been beaten by Celine. Then she went on to speak about the isolation that had been her life for three years. She talked about guilt, shame and humiliation. And about being a victim.

She glanced into the audience at Kim, who had been beaten by Barbara. Sitting next to her was Vanessa, who had been beaten by Pat. They both gave her the thumbs-up sign and she went on.

"One night, after running through a rainstorm, bruised and bleeding, to find refuge with my dear friend Kristie, I decided not to be a victim anymore. I decided to find myself again, and I finally did in the faces of nineteen other women just like me."

The room was silent.

She recited statistics about lesbian domestic violence and the lack of formal research to determine the real extent of its existence. She talked about the need of the gay and lesbian community to grapple with same-sex abuse openly and heatedly, peer-to-peer. And, finally, to emphasize that very point, she spoke graphically about her own abuse nightmare.

"Let me tell you what was in my closet. Let me throw out into this public arena for everyone to hear the private, hellish passions I lived for two years. I was abused physically — slapped, punched, kicked. I was forced to participate in sex against my will. I endured lies, insults, humiliation, blackmail. My life was threatened with knives, baseball bats, shovels and fireplace tools. I was taken for car rides I never thought I'd survive. My friends and family were alienated. Everything I did was wrong — and everything that was wrong was about me. And, while I endured all of this, I heard every excuse known to man. The abuser in my life was once abused. She had a traumatic childhood. She had a drinking problem. She was under a great deal of stress at work. She couldn't control her anger. I tried to understand it, tried to view it all with compassion."

Sara paused and looked out over the audience.

"But her excuses were only that, excuses. There are no excuses for violence or abuse. There are only choices. To acknowledge that you have a problem, go to counseling, deal with your anger and stop abusing." Sara clenched her fists to keep her hands from shaking. "And let me also say this. If you are an abuse victim, there are finally choices for you as well. To talk, to get support, to find out about your legal rights. To begin to live again."

Sara folded up her notes. "For two years I gave my life over to someone else. Today, along with many other women, I've started my life over. It's been a long journey and it's far from over. But tonight, I can see to feel again. And I feel great. Thank you."

The applause lasted for several minutes. When Sara turned to leave the podium, Dr. Langford was waiting.

"Sara, I'm so proud of you." The doctor hugged her gently. "Thank you."

After the final keynote speaker, the crowd from the dinner and meeting moved slowly outside into the warm, muggy evening air.

Kristie grabbed Sara's hand, intertwining her fingers with her own. "Love you, baby. Never been more proud."

"Thanks. I love you, too."

Kristie kissed her hand. "Coming by the club tonight?"

Sara looked off to her right. Jasmin was waiting for her by the hotel steps. "I don't know."

Kristie looked in the same direction. "Ahh, I see. Someone's waiting for you."

"Yes."

Kristie nodded and smiled. "Then you should go."

Sara reached out and hugged Kristie as tight as she could. As always, it was hard to let go. "Kris, I want you to know —"

"Shh, baby. Not now. Remember, you can see to feel again. And what you're feeling is waiting for you right over there." Kristie cocked her head in Jasmin's direction. "See ya later, kiddo."

"Later."

Jasmin looked as beautiful as the night sky. Her dark skin was a lovely contrast against the white linen jacket she wore.

"Want to take a walk with me?" Sara asked.

"Where to?"

Sara looked up toward the Westin building. "Thought you might like to see that beautiful view again."

"What a wonderful idea."

Sara pulled Jasmin close, wrapping her arms around her. She could see the Nation's Bank Plaza, the Westin, Peachtree Center and the other buildings that strung the city skyline together. She pointed toward the skyline and Jasmin's gaze followed. The view was God-like. The view was Atlanta — and it was finally home.

FOURTH DOWN by Kate Calloway. 240 pp. 4th Cassidy James mystery. ISBN 1-56280-205-4 11.95

A MOMENT'S INDISCRETION by Peggy J. Herring. 176 pp. There's a fine line between love and lust . . . ISBN 1-56280-194-5 11.95

CITY LIGHTS/COUNTRY CANDLES by Penny Hayes. 208 pp. About the women she has known . . . ISBN 1-56280-195-3 11.95

POSSESSIONS by Kaye Davis. 240 pp. 2nd Maris Middleton mystery. ISBN 1-56280-192-9 11.95

A QUESTION OF LOVE by Saxon Bennett. 208 pp. Every woman is granted one great love. ISBN 1-56280-205-4 11.95

RHYTHM TIDE by Frankie J. Jones. 160 pp. . . . to desire passionately and be passionately desired. ISBN 1-56280-189-9 11.95

PENN VALLEY PHOENIX by Janet McClellan. 208 pp. 2nd Tru North Mystery. ISBN 1-56280-200-3 11.95

BY RESERVATION ONLY by Jackie Calhoun. 240 pp. A chance for true happiness. ISBN 1-56280-191-0 11.95

OLD BLACK MAGIC by Jaye Maiman. 272 pp. 9th Robin Miller mystery. ISBN 1-56280-175-9 11.95

LEGACY OF LOVE by Marianne K. Martin. 240 pp. Women will do anything for her . . . ISBN 1-56280-184-8 11.95

LETTING GO by Ann O'Leary. 160 pp. Laura, at 39, in love with 23-year-old Kate. ISBN 1-56280-183-X 11.95

LADY BE GOOD edited by Barbara Grier and Christine Cassidy. 288 pp. Erotic stories by Naiad Press authors. ISBN 1-56280-180-5 14.95

CHAIN LETTER by Claire McNab. 288 pp. 9th Carol Ashton mystery. ISBN 1-56280-181-3 11.95

NIGHT VISION by Laura Adams. 256 pp. Erotic fantasy romance by "famous" author. ISBN 1-56280-182-1 11.95

SEA TO SHINING SEA by Lisa Shapiro. 256 pp. Unable to resist the raging passion . . . ISBN 1-56280-177-5 11.95

THIRD DEGREE by Kate Calloway. 224 pp. 3rd Cassidy James mystery. ISBN 1-56280-185-6 11.95

WHEN THE DANCING STOPS by Therese Szymanski. 272 pp. 1st Brett Higgins mystery. ISBN 1-56280-186-4 11.95

PHASES OF THE MOON by Julia Watts. 192 pp. . . . hungry for everything life has to offer. ISBN 1-56280-176-7 11.95

BABY IT'S COLD by Jaye Maiman. 256 pp. 5th Robin Miller mystery. ISBN 1-56280-156-2 10.95

CLASS REUNION by Linda Hill. 176 pp. The girl from her past . . . ISBN 1-56280-178-3 11.95

DREAM LOVER by Lyn Denison. 224 pp. A soft, sensuous, romantic fantasy. ISBN 1-56280-173-1 11.95

FORTY LOVE by Diana Simmonds. 288 pp. Joyous, heart-warming romance. ISBN 1-56280-171-6 11.95

IN THE MOOD by Robbi Sommers. 160 pp. The queen of erotic tension! ISBN 1-56280-172-4 11.95

SWIMMING CAT COVE by Lauren Douglas. 192 pp. 2nd Allison O'Neil Mystery. ISBN 1-56280-168-6 11.95

THE LOVING LESBIAN by Claire McNab and Sharon Gedan. 240 pp. Explore the experiences that make lesbian love unique. ISBN 1-56280-169-4 14.95

COURTED by Celia Cohen. 160 pp. Sparkling romantic encounter. ISBN 1-56280-166-X 11.95

SEASONS OF THE HEART by Jackie Calhoun. 240 pp. Romance through the years. ISBN 1-56280-167-8 11.95

K. C. BOMBER by Janet McClellan. 208 pp. 1st Tru North mystery. ISBN 1-56280-157-0 11.95

LAST RITES by Tracey Richardson. 192 pp. 1st Stevie Houston mystery. ISBN 1-56280-164-3 11.95

EMBRACE IN MOTION by Karin Kallmaker. 256 pp. A whirlwind love affair. ISBN 1-56280-165-1 11.95

HOT CHECK by Peggy J. Herring. 192 pp. Will workaholic Alice fall for guitarist Ricky? ISBN 1-56280-163-5 11.95

OLD TIES by Saxon Bennett. 176 pp. Can Cleo surrender to a passionate new love? ISBN 1-56280-159-7 11.95

LOVE ON THE LINE by Laura DeHart Young. 176 pp. Will Stef win Kay's heart? ISBN 1-56280-162-7 11.95

DEVIL'S LEG CROSSING by Kaye Davis. 192 pp. 1st Maris Middleton mystery. ISBN 1-56280-158-9 11.95

COSTA BRAVA by Marta Balletbo Coll. 144 pp. Read the book, see the movie! ISBN 1-56280-153-8 11.95

MEETING MAGDALENE & OTHER STORIES by Marilyn Freeman. 144 pp. Read the book, see the movie! ISBN 1-56280-170-8 11.95

SECOND FIDDLE by Kate 208 pp. 2nd P.I. Cassidy James mystery. ISBN 1-56280-169-6 11.95

These are just a few of the many Naiad Press titles — we are the oldest and largest lesbian/feminist publishing company in the world. We also offer an enormous selection of lesbian video products. Please request a complete catalog. We offer personal service; we encourage and welcome direct mail orders from individuals who have limited access to bookstores carrying our publications.